WARNING

This book contains sexually explicit scenes and adult language. It may be considered offensive to some readers. This book is for sale to adults ONLY.

* * * * * * * * * * * * * * * * *

Please store your files wisely where they cannot be accessed by underage readers.

ISBN-13: 978-1988083926
ISBN-10: 1988083923

Other Books by Darla Dunbar:

<u>The Romeo Alpha BBW Paranormal Shifter Romance Series</u> (This series precedes the "<u>Romeo Alpha Blood Lines Romance Series</u>")

Amanda Walker thinks that she has a normal and boring life. That is until after her 24th birthday. Everything changes when she meets the man who says he was supposed to be her husband. Denying everything the man says, she fights him every step of the way. But after he kidnaps her, Amanda discovers that there are some things about her family that her parents kept a secret all these years. Among the history of the family she learns secrets she thought only happened in story books. Can Amanda tell the difference between truth and lies or is she this mysterious woman that holds the key to a legacy?

<u>The Alpha Feud BBW Paranormal Shifter Romance Series</u>

Eliza's life consisted of reporting on boring, crowd-pleasing events, like their country livestock fair. With the arrival of two handsome brothers, the lives of Eliza and her best friend, Melissa, are shaken to the core. For Eliza, the arrival of this new man becomes a test of her relationship with her current boyfriend, who she's been happily living with for over six years. Does Hayden, a complete stranger, really wield the power to make Eliza reconsider her relationship with Andrew?

The Alpha Packed BBW Paranormal Shifter Romance Series

Darlene has led a quiet life since suffering through a terrible break-up. She wants nothing more than to spend her time in front of the TV, away from any sort of trouble. But all that goes down the drain when handsome, rugged and rough Idris comes into her life. He is a werewolf on the lookout for his missing pack leader. Darlene quickly finds herself pulled towards this mysterious man and at the same time finds herself falling deeper and deeper into the world of the supernatural.

The Daemon Paranormal Romance Chronicles

The daemon infighting can only be stopped when a strong leader emerges to calm the different factions. Juno appears to be at the heart of the conflict. Things become complicated when Phoebe and Supay try to negotiate with the siren, Juno. The love triangle among Phoebe, Supay and Apollo become tense when Juno's meddling threatens to destroy any romance that develops.

The Mind Talker Paranormal Romance Series

Ananda finds herself on the run and she's not alone. With help from Jared, a stranger that she just met, the two evade capture by an organization that is intent on hunting her kind. Ananda and Jared are able to read minds. When an unfortunate incident happened involving a disturbed individual that resulted in the death of his schoolmates, the secret organization decided to take action.

Valtina is stuck in Middle World, unable to pass on to The Afterlife. In order to redeem herself from past deeds done, she must help bring romance back into the world and stop The Dark Side from destroying love in its entirety. Following orders issued by Ladaya and armed with a leather satchel filled with the appropriate tools and weapons, Valtina embraces each mission with enthusiasm.

Get the latest update on new releases from the author at:

https://darladunbar.com/newsletter/

This book is Part Four of the "<u>Romeo Alpha Blood Lines Romance Series</u>" and follows twenty-four years after "<u>The Romeo Alpha BBW Paranormal Shifter Romance Series</u>"

1 - Blood Lines

Twenty-four years have passed in relative peace for Amanda and Romeo. They've raised five children into adulthood and are thoroughly enjoying their lives as the Alpha King and Queen of the werewolves. At twenty-four, Sarina is just stepping into her powers and will be ripe for mating when her birthday comes in two weeks. What no one knows is the danger that lurks just outside their tight knit community. Romeo has made peace with the other clans and has enjoyed that peace, but it will all come crashing down around him when his oldest daughter comes of age to take a mate.

2 - Alpha Infiltration

Brody is an attentive and loving mate and Sarina finds herself engulfed by the love of her family. When things start to change with the twins though, Sarina finds herself torn in two. She loves Brody in a way she's never loved another man, human or wolf. When he shows signs of the dark void, however, she can't decide whether to run from him or to him. She's frightened for both of her sons and struggles with her own mortality.

3 - Alpha Bait

Lilith is on the loose, plotting and planning with Fenris to take down the Delta pack and its alpha, Romeo. Sarina and Brody have their work cut out for them in order to stop the hostile takeover. With their wedding on the horizon, both feel compelled to spend time with their family even as danger lurks around every corner. When the twin babies, Jedidiah and Brody Jr., go missing, all hands are on deck to search for the leaders of the next generation of the Delta pack. And as Sarina and Brody dig deeper into Lilith's past, especially where Romeo is concerned, they find a mind twisted by deception and an overly unhealthy obsession with power.

4 - Alpha Strategy

With Lilith's soul separated from her body, Romeo and Amanda are bent on seeing her body destroyed so that she never comes back again. What they've forgotten in the meantime is that Lilith wasn't alone in her desire over control of the Delta pack and Romeo. Sarina and Brody are finally enjoying a quiet life, not that they expect it to last long. Their wedding, a source of great stress, is just weeks away. With all that's going on though, Sarina wonders if she'll ever be able to legally wed her mate.

5 - Alpha Revelation

Lilith has haunted the Traverse family since the beginning but her obsession with the reigning alpha and his immediate family is more than Romeo's eldest daughter can stand. In a twisted allegiance with her first mate, Fenris, Lilith has caused unbearable pain to the Delta pack's community and now she has gone as far as to make a deal with the Devil. She has comfortably inhabited Sarina's body, playing wife to Brody and mother to the couple's twin boys. Digging her way up from Hell wasn't easy, but Sarina harnesses powers that rival even those of her mother.

Alpha Romeo Blood Lines Romance Series

Alpha Strategy

Book Four

By Darla Dunbar

Table of Contents

Chapter One

ROMEO TRAVERSE waited just outside the woods, his shoulder and hip still ached from the silver-tipped arrows his wife, Amanda, had removed less than four hours before. His pride, however, would take longer to heal. As the alpha of the Delta pack, taking two arrows in battle scored him deeper than the tips could ever hope to penetrate. Still, he had his beautiful wife to thank for the healing that was already working its magic. Without it, he'd never have gotten this far. Still in his wolf, Romeo sat scanning the tree line. He'd brought everyone from his pack who'd been available to help. Gina, his niece, had stayed behind with Sarina, her older cousin and his first born. Brody, Sarina's husband, had also stayed behind with four soldier wolves to guard his two grandsons. As the youngest heirs to the Delta pack, Jedidiah and Brody Jr. couldn't be risked and with one attempt already foiled to use them as bait, Romeo wasn't about to take another chance with them by removing their father. He'd spared the four wolves without hesitation.

His middle son, Wade, had made the trip as had his two youngest twins, Shawna and Joshua. Shawna was a ways back in the wooded area of their territory helping her mother take care of two wolves who'd come from somewhere in the woods. How they'd missed their presence all this time was a concern for another day as Romeo waited.

The arrows that had sunk into his flesh had come from the direction that Romeo was now exploring and he would find the shooter. As for whether or not that shooter was alone, well, he'd just have to figure that out along the way. And figure it out he would. The safety of his entire pack depended on ending Fenris once and for all.

Sitting on his haunches to breathe for a minute, Romeo thought back to all they'd gone through; the very first werewolf had a penchant for ruling everything.

Thankfully, the Delta pack had rallied and come back even stronger after Fenris and his pack had wiped out several of the male wolves' families. Nearly a hundred women and children had died that night and it had crippled Romeo's numbers, not to mention what it had done to the pack's morale. Over the last few months, Romeo and his entire family had worked themselves to the bone to keep those male wolves from defecting and going after Fenris on their own. He was glad to have all of them with him tonight. Three nights away from the full moon, he needed every wolf he could get for this fight, especially if he was going to end it once and for all.

The arrows he'd received were a precursor, he knew, to what was coming. Fenris had wolves under his command who'd take on the fight and keep going. Romeo could only hope that Fenris didn't have enough.

If any other packs came to join him, Romeo knew it'd
be bloody and brutal, something he wanted to avoid at
all costs. He wasn't afraid of the fight, but he didn't
want to waste the lives of his pack members just to
snuff out a wolf who should have died eons ago... one
who'd caused more than his fair share of trouble. The
mere fact that he'd planted a decoy, a wolf who'd
disguised himself as Sarina Traverse's own mate,
Brody, galled Romeo more than he wanted to admit.
And to think that worthless black magician Dankar had
been able to pull off such a ruse.

Romeo knew better than anyone that war was
personal, from the infantry all the way up to the
decision makers. Just as he knew that Fenris had more
than overstepped his bounds when that young man had
done his dirty deed. He wasn't one to hold a grudge, but
in Fenris' case, he'd certainly make an exception. And
as if Fenris wasn't enough to deal with these past
months, they'd had to put up with Lilith, the woman
who created the werewolves in the first place. It pricked
his ego considerably to have to admit that she had
duped him. Consumed by black magic, she'd found a
way to crawl back from the pits of Hell and somehow
managed to slither inside Brody's mind. It wasn't long
before she'd found her body. It had cost Romeo his son
and now he owed Fenris for Jason's death as well.

"Sir."

Romeo turned to see one of his generals standing at his side and quickly put away thoughts of the past. He tilted his head and the man continued

"Your scouts have returned with a count."

Romeo knew the change would hurt and likely drain his energy even more, but he also knew that he needed to get the information correct the first time around. It took mere minutes for the shift to complete and Romeo was thankful for the young man who tossed him a pair of shorts to put on.

"What's the report?" Romeo asked, knowing they needed to formulate a plan of attack that would end Fenris' pack forever.

"There's some twenty-five archers posted around the area sir. Some I recognized but plenty I didn't. I don't mean to assume sir, but I'm almost sure Fenris has asked for and received outside help. He's never been dumb in the past and I doubt he'd slip up now, sir."

"Thank you," Romeo said, dismissing the young man with a wave of his hand. The young scout took his original place in the pack and Romeo turned to his top four wolves. "Alright, obviously we need these wolves taken out before we see about attacking the wolves inside the caves. None of us here have been inside, save me, and that will need some attention to detail. Right now though, I want our archers to worry about the twenty-five wolves that our scout saw. That's Fenris' front line of defense and that's where we'll strike first."

Chapter Two

Fenris sat in his chambers looking at a map of New Delta. He'd plotted out his approach and knew exactly when and where to strike. The last attack had gone exactly as planned and would make a huge difference in giving him the upper hand. It had not only crippled their numbers, but had also put a massive dent in their morale. That combination would give his pack a big hand up in winning the game they were obviously playing. He intended to win, even if it meant his life.

When someone knocked on his door, he looked up from the map and said, "Come in."

"I've positioned the men in a perimeter around the caves. A report just came back to me that a man was pegged with two silver-tipped arrows," said the commander at the door.

"And who was this man?"

"Initial reports claimed he was Romeo Traverse, sir. But the latest reports aren't sure exactly who he was."

"I want whoever said he was Romeo Traverse brought to me immediately," said Fenris.

"Yes, sir."

Fenris paced the confines of his chambers as he waited. So Romeo Traverse had finally come to his turf. It'd taken him long enough, Fenris thought. He'd been dogging Romeo since before Lilith showed up. He knew now that his enemy was a formidable one. Not every alpha would have waited this long to form an attack, especially given what he'd done to their pack weeks earlier. He remembered the first time he'd met Lilith as if it was yesterday.

At the Beginning

The woods smelled of fall as dusk fell and fresh dew covered the ground. The Delta was teeming with life as Fenris walked along a worn path, his hand lightly holding Christy's. "I had a wonderful time tonight," she said, smiling up at him.

"I couldn't have asked for a better night," he agreed. "The stars looked incredible and even the crowd wasn't terrible."

"I expected there to be a lot more people," she continued. "Especially considering the President was visiting."

"Me too," Fenris agreed. A low, feral growl from the woods made them stop in their tracks. When a beautiful woman stepped onto the path, he dropped Christy's hand instantly. "Hello."

"Hello handsome," the beautiful woman grinned. "You'll have to excuse me. I… I'm a bit hungry tonight."

"We… we don't have any food as we just came from dinner," he said. "We can help you find some place that will feed you."

"Oh that won't be necessary," she grinned. "I'll keep for a while yet. I don't suppose you two would be interested in a tryst of sorts."

"A tryst?" Christy scoffed. "My boyfriend is walking me home as any gentleman would do for his girl."

"A girl, are you?" the woman said, a sneer on her face. Fenris couldn't look away from her, even when Christy tugged on his arm. "Perhaps your boyfriend needs to find himself a woman, instead of trifling around with girls."

"I'm a grown woman and I don't need to be chastised by the likes of you." In the blink of an eye, the mysterious woman was standing in front of him and Fenris could have sworn he saw deadly sharp fangs when she grinned at him. Then her head turned toward Christy.

"Well if you're a woman as you say, then why isn't your boyfriend telling me to leave?"

"He's a gentleman as I said," Christy said, moving closer to Fenris, who hadn't moved an inch since she'd stepped onto the road.

"Is he?" the woman laughed. "Well then, he wouldn't be interested in dropping you off at home and spending some time with me then. I suppose I should be on my way. I've got things to do, men mainly, but still."

"Wait," Fenris found himself saying. He could feel Christy's hand clamp onto his arm as if she'd been cemented to him, but he couldn't help himself. The woman, whoever she was, simply couldn't be ignored.

"Yes?"

"I... Christy I'll make sure you get home safe and sound, but I... I can't see you anymore."

"You're going to dump me just like that because she's offering you sex?"

He could hear the derision in her voice but it didn't matter, nothing mattered except the woman who stood in front of him. "It's not that simple and I don't expect you to understand at all."

"Allow me," the woman said, taking hold of Christy's arm.

"Hey!" Christy yelled. Fenris blinked and the women were gone, almost as if they'd never been there. The next time he blinked, the mysterious woman was back, without breaking so much as a sweat.

"How did you... where is she?"

"She's at home, safe and sound. I was after a much bigger fish," the beauty said. Fenris couldn't remember the last time, if ever, that he'd seen a woman so beautiful. Long, curling, dark hair, porcelain skin that beckoned to him. She'd painted her lips the color of ripe red roses and when she smiled, Fenris could feel his loins tighten.

"Come on," she smiled.

Her home was quaint and while simple on the outside, he could tell she had expensive tastes by the way she decorated.

"Your home is lovely," he said.

"Flattery isn't necessary," she said, stripping off the coat she'd worn earlier. Fenris turned to see her and nearly swallowed his tongue when she stood before him naked.

"Christ," Fenris breathed.

"He won't have me now," she chuckled. "My name's Lilith."

"Fenris," he stammered. She moved closer and Fenris fought not to step back from her.

"Alright, Fenris," she whispered. Her stunning blue eyes seemed to look past him as her mouth curved in a soft smile. "Well, are you planning on standing there all night?"

"No, ugh, no ma'am."

"I'm nineteen, Fenris, hardly old enough to be called ma'am," she giggled. "How about we just start out with a kiss?"

"A kiss," he fumbled.

"Surely you're not afraid of a kiss?"

Her smile widened as her hand came up to touch his cheek. Then her thumb ran over his bottom lip and Fenris had the urge to bite her, to leave a mark on her perfect silky skin. Gripping her arms, he pulled her closer, pressing his mouth to hers and closing in the space between their bodies. Her hands came around his waist and slid down to cup his ass. She pressed herself impossibly closer, bringing her breasts tight against his chest.

"Well," she breathed as she pulled back. "There's some fire in you after all."

"I can't think around you."

"Thinking is overrated anyways," she laughed. He couldn't exactly argue with her. Taking her hand, he led her to the bedroom, the only room in her house with a door. Fenris closed the door and enjoyed standing in the moonlight shining through the window, watching her. He'd known the moment he saw her that she'd change his life. He'd wanted her, wanted what she was plainly offering, but there was so much more, so much she wasn't saying. That was what he couldn't wait to discover.

<<<>>>

Lilith had been with enough human men to know she'd found an incredible specimen. Over the last two centuries, her nights had been filled with enough lust to fill an ocean. There'd been some love, not much to speak of, but some. In the beginning, when she'd wanted to deny what had happened to her, she'd tried to love a man. Eventually though, he'd noticed that she never seemed to eat much and that she wanted to sleep all day and be up all night long. She left at odd hours of the night and came back with torn clothes, smelling of sex and blood. She'd tried to explain, but no explanation would convince a human man to stay with what she'd become. There wasn't even a name for her, whatever she was now. She never aged, she never ached with discomfort and even if she managed to hurt herself, she healed miraculously, fast and well. Except when it involved sunlight. Sunlight was a tricky bitch if she'd ever met one. That and holy water. She hadn't had many chances to come into contact with that particular liquid as she avoided churches and holy places like the plague, but still, she'd encountered enough to know that too much could harm her.

Ever since being bitten by a couple of wolves a few nights prior, however, strange things had happened to her. The night before she'd felt odd, powerful changes happening to her body. The change was breathtaking at first. Her bones had broken and somehow shifted into a form she wasn't even sure she was familiar with. Even now, when she moved her mouth and jaw she could still feel the effects of that elongated muzzle, if that even was what it was. It didn't seem to matter really though, whether she was in this human form or the other. Her thirst for blood was the same, insatiable.

Now she had a man to share it with, one who didn't startle easily. She'd looked into his eyes and known from that instant, he would be her first change. She wasn't quite sure how it would all work, but there was an urge in her to have someone, someone like her, to share this existence with. She wanted to have someone who understood her completely. Fenris was going to be that someone.

"Tell me you want me," said Lilith.

"I dumped my girlfriend to be with you," Fenris said, his shining blue eyes completely too innocent for her.

"Yes you did," she said, smiling. Crawling across the bed to him, Lilith grinned. "And I'll make it worth your while."

"Do you always boast this proudly?"

"Only when I can back it up with performance," she said, chuckling. "Do you want what I have to offer?"

She could see he did. Even if he didn't say it, his eyes did with the way they lit with need and pure male appreciation; she knew he'd be hers.

She took him down slowly, running her warm lips over his, playfully seductive. She nipped him here and there, tasting the different flavors of his flesh and letting him know the need he stirred in her. He wanted to lead, she could feel it in the way his body hummed against hers. His powerful form covered hers, sinking them both into her huge bed. Still, the animal, or animals in her needed to dominate and soon each showed its true nature. Stronger by far, Lilith flipped Fenris over and straddled him, delight lighting his eyes as he cupped her breasts. She took him into her in one long stroke, impaling herself fully and enjoying his impressive fullness. The way he slid into her made her body tighten in all the right places. More than human or not, she had needs and Fenris was well on his way to meeting them. Rocking her hips, Lilith moaned as his cock flexed inside her warm pussy. She knew hunger, the kind that could suck your soul out of your body, but this craving was one only a man could satisfy. Nothing she did herself came close to this. Taking the edge off a need was one thing, but meeting it fully was an entirely different matter. Lilith knew the moment she'd smelled Fenris that he was ripe for what she needed to give him. It only made her hotter knowing that soon he'd be like her, able to give and take like her.

Pressing her hands down on his shoulders, Lilith let her long hair fall in a curtain around them as she brought her wet mouth down to his. He was building inside of her and she wanted that moment when he teetered on the precipice of completion to be the moment she took him. His change would be her greatest triumph.

Sliding her tongue between his full lips, she tasted his arousal as his hands gripped her hips. He pulled her down, thrusting his hard cock deeper into her. Over and over again he filled her so that her breath came in short, choppy gasps. Pulling back, Lilith ran her tongue over the curved, strained muscles of Fenris' neck as he exploded inside her. In that moment, while he came inside of her, a different need filled her veins and she sank her teeth, sharpened to a killing point, into the hot flesh there.

Blood spewed into her mouth, the hot, life giving spurt of it teasing the back of her throat as she tasted him. His howl only fueled her need and she feasted on him. Drained as much as she could without taking his life, Lilith sliced her tongue until it bled deeply and slid it between his mumbling lips as her own orgasm slammed through her at the thought of having him forever. Fenris would be hers for eternity.

Chapter Three

Fenris brought himself back from the past with a hard shake of his head. Every now and then, he could still feel that moment when he'd woken to eternal life. It was like being a baby again, having to learn everything that had changed, knowing he was somehow, strangely different from who'd he been in just his human form. His first change had been excruciatingly difficult, especially because Lilith had scarcely been there to explain what the hell she'd done to him.

Now she was dead and he was left, again, to clean up her mess. Being a man and an alpha wolf, he knew that his pack needed the female to survive, but man, they could be useless, destructive bitches sometimes.

"You wished to see me, sir?" asked a young wolf who just arrived.

"Yes, my boy." Fenris drew the young wolf closer. "I'd very much like you to tell me how you knew it was Romeo Traverse who was shot by our archers."

"I got a good look at his face, sir."

"Uh-huh. And what happened when he was shot?"

"He stepped back into the forest, sir. But not before your boy got him again."

"And you're positive, as in, I can filet your skin from your body if you're wrong, positive?"

"Absolutely, sir."

"Excellent," Fenris grinned. He loved accurate information, but there was a part of him that enjoyed the torture when one of his wolves slipped up.

You're a sick son-of-a-bitch, Fenris thought to himself as he looked over the New Delta map again. He looked at the wooded perimeter that met the mountains to his north and wondered how many wolves Romeo had brought with him. He'd certainly brought the men who'd lost their wives and children. They'd fight as if the Devil chased them for sure, a fight Fenris was very much anticipating.

<<<>>>

Rolling up his map, Fenris gathered his pack and those who'd come to join him, together. "We've waited what seems like forever, for tonight," he started. "The Traverse line has been a thorn in my side since its creation and tonight… tonight we'll crush them under our feet!"

Roars, howls and applause drowned him out, making him pause for a moment. Holding up a hand, he quieted the crowd. "The wolf that takes down as many of the Delta pack as possible will have considerable privilege among my pack, but I want to make it crystal clear that Romeo Traverse is mine and mine alone. I will take down the alpha of this pack as it is my right. If anyone has a problem with that, we can discuss it in a minute. Otherwise, let's get into position!"

No one argued with the old man as he continued his speech. There wasn't a point as everyone knew that if they overstepped their bounds, he'd see them executed without delay.

There were some murmurs within the crowd. "You think it's really Romeo Traverse's Delta pack out there?"

"Hell no," a young wolf said, with a little too much confidence. "Romeo Traverse may be impulsive but he's not dumb. If it was his pack, we'd have some serious action by now. Whoever said it was his pack, I'd hate to be him come morning."

"Still, it'll be a nice reward to claim the most kills and whatever privilege Fenris has up his sleeve."

"You honestly think he's going to reward anyone but himself?"

"Why not? It gives us all an incentive to fight, doesn't it?"

"An incentive sure. But what about when it comes to collecting the reward? There's no way he gives privilege to anyone but himself. He'll never give up his alpha position or anything that elevates anyone to his level. The reward will either suck ass or be reserved for him."

The two wolves found their positions near the main entrance to the caves, hoping they'd be the one to win the day, despite their banter about the worthiness of the reward they'd be given.

<<◇>>

Amanda Traverse sat outside the small cabin she couldn't see and talked with her youngest daughter, Shawna. "It doesn't bode well for our kind if there's a cabin here that I can't see. Even with my powers, I can't seem to find even the slightest edge of it. I can't even feel it when I stretch my hand out."

"What are you going to do?"

"I'll have to ask you and Sarina to see to Carly's comfort. She needs to take it easy during these last few weeks. The baby she carries depends on it."

"But what about the twins? There's no way Sarina will leave them, even if Lilith really is gone."

"I'll keep the twins safe. If we're going to keep Carly and her baby safe and healthy, she'll need round the clock care until she delivers. I can't do it myself, since I can't see the cabin and once she's inside, I won't be able see her either."

"You have to admit, Mama. That's weird. Even your powers aren't helpful and that's just bizarre."

"Tell me about it," Amanda said, obviously uneasy about the situation. She'd never had anything be so closed to her. Whoever or whatever was protecting this cabin from her sight must have a pretty powerful reason to do so. She couldn't say it didn't irk her a little bit to know that her powers were limited, especially on Delta pack land. "We need to make sure no one disturbs them."

"So far it seems as if no one has even noticed that they're here. You don't suppose we're in some sort of bubble of protection do you?"

"The force field we created during the last battle we fought would have worn off by now. If it's a spell from someone else, I think, I hope I'd be able to deduce that and I don't feel anything. Other than that, I can't imagine any other reason I shouldn't be able to see this place. Whoever or whatever is keeping this place from my vision needs me to figure out why."

"Do you think there'd be anyone actively seeking this cabin out?"

"I'm not sure. When it comes to this cabin, I feel completely in the dark, no pun intended. As far as we know, I'm the only one who can't see it. That makes it an easy target for anyone who might want a place to hide out. The original force field we created can be recreated, but I'm not sure it can be extended to last longer. That and I'm not sure Brandt and Carly are going to want to be trapped inside. Moving in and out is only possible for the ones who make the force field. Anyone else is either trapped inside or kept out by it."

"I can talk to Aunt Pen about it. See if she can look into how we extend that force field. Maybe we can cast it larger and give Carly some space to move around outside the cabin."

"Maybe, but we need to make sure she understands as well that she needs to rest."

"I doubt that'll be a problem. Not with Brandt hovering over her."

"Probably not, but to be safe, we'll make sure to tell them again."

Amanda knew that regardless of the cabin and why she couldn't see it, they needed to induct Brandt, Carly and their children into the Delta pack. It was dangerous to be leaderless, especially when living on another pack's land. Standing, she relied on Shawna to be her eyes and smiled when Brandt came into view. As he descended the stairs, or what she assumed were stairs, Amanda felt a wave of nausea inducing evil sweep over her. Immediately the hair on the back of her neck stood on end. "Where did you say you came from?"

"I was part of Fenris' pack until I met Carly."

"And where did Carly come from?"

"She belonged to a pack that has territory farther east of the Delta. From what she's told me, they're settled close to the Atlantic Ocean."

"I think her pack is looking for her and if my assumptions are right, they're close, much too close."

"You're sure?"

"Right now, in this place, I'm not sure of anything except that you all need to come with me, now.

Whoever is shielding this place isn't someone you want to tussle with."

"But she can't—"

"We'll figure out a way," Amanda said, ending the discussion. She waited anxiously as Brandt came out carrying Carly, who looked less than comfortable. "I'm very sorry about all of this Carly, but you're in severe danger… you *and* the child you carry. Shawna, can you hold one of the little ones?"

Amanda turned to head toward the place where she'd left Romeo, grabbing the other twin as she did so. If there were any of her wolves left, they'd mask Carly's scent until Amanda could get her family within the wider protection of the Delta pack. "Demetri," Shawna called to a wolf who stood point, looking for movement.

"Shawna," he said, bowing slightly.

Amanda didn't miss the blush that stained her daughter's cheeks. At twenty-one she was still too young to breed, but that didn't mean she didn't have needs. It'd be a conversation for later.

"What can we do?" Demetri asked.

"We need you to mask this woman's scent and that of her children. Her former pack is looking for her and I believe they've allied themselves with Fenris in order to find her. If they find out she's within our ranks, she'll be in even greater danger," said Amanda.

"Understood," the young man said. He stepped closer to the woman Brandt carried and looking into her eyes, pressed his hands to her heavily swollen abdomen.

"What's he doing?" Brandt asked, understandably nervous.

"He's absorbing Carly's scent. When he's done, he'll do the same to your children. This will make them virtually odorless until we can get them home. You'll stay at the main mansion until this threat has passed. I should also tell you that my daughter and son-in-law are also there with their twins. It may make for an uncomfortable stay at first, but without it, her pack will find her and I fear what they'll do when they figure out where she is. Not to mention, that she'd borne children."

"Won't it be easy to just assume she's in the Delta pack, considering we're in Delta pack territory?" asked Brandt.

"Not necessarily. Fenris, as you said, doesn't know where you are. Without that connection, he has virtually no idea who Carly is. He's simply giving them aid because without it he'd have no one to fight."

"Alright," Brandt said, finally relenting.

Amanda and Shawna moved quickly now, getting Brandt and Carly to the main Traverse mansion within two hours of leaving the cabin.

"Is there something I should know about you and Demetri Benikov?" Amanda asked, turning to her youngest daughter.

"Why?" Shawna's eyes widened when she heard her mother mention Demetri's name.

"Because I'm a woman who knows what the look he gave you means and more importantly, I'm your mother."

Amanda heard her daughter sigh and inwardly cringed. "He's more than a passing flirtation, for me."

"And for him?" Amanda questioned, gently.

"I'm not sure how he feels exactly. He's a gentleman, respectful, kind, generous. He's what I want in a mate, in the future father of my children. I just don't know how to get him to tell me what's in his heart."

"Well," Amanda smiled. "In due time, all of that will come out. If he feels anything of what I saw in his face when he looked at you, you're going to be a very happy breeder when your time comes."

"Can I wed before my breeding season starts?"

"You always were my go-getter. Always jumping at the bit for the next thrill," Amanda smiled. "I'd caution you to take this slowly. Enjoy this time with Demetri. If he's the gentleman you say he is, he'll wait for the time you need to be ready."

"It's me who needs to be talked into waiting," Shawna chuckled. "Demetri tends to get this deer-in-the-headlights look in his eyes whenever I mention mating or breeding, or anything related to settling down."

"Most men do," Amanda laughed. "Although your father was not one of them. Of course he was quite a bit older than Demetri is now. By the time I came into his life, your father was more than ready to settle down, mostly because I had come into season and he knew the only way to protect me was for us to mate."

"Wasn't your first time scary?"

"Not scary, really," Amanda explained. "I was nervous, unsure of myself and him. I had no expectations and no knowledge about what was happening, other than what I'd learned in school. Let me assure you, the actual act is so much more than anyone can describe."

"And father?"

"He was this massive bundle of pent up frustration mixed heavily with a touch of anger and even some resentment. I'm sure he was cursing Aunt Mabel for leaving her estate to me. Despite wanting me, needing me even, your father wasn't as confident as he wanted me to believe. He was like a bully inside a handsome man."

"My dad was a bully?" Shawna asked with a giggle as they stepped onto her home's immediate property.

"If he wasn't huffing about one thing, he was puffing about something else. Always pushing me along as if I didn't have the sense to decide where I wanted my life to go."

"I'd never let any man, wolf or not, tell me how to live my life," said Shawna, her defiance for her independence making itself known.

"You can understand my predicament," Amanda said, grinning. "Suffice it to say we eventually figured things out between us. Being intimate helped a great deal with all of that because we could finally sit down and talk, think, without the static sexual tension between us. Not that I'm advocating you should give yourself to Demetri. With three years still before you're ready to breed, you have plenty of time to figure out what both of you need and want. There's no need to rush things right now and I can assure you, when the right man comes along, you'll know."

"But you and Dad—"

"It took us a little while, but considering the alternative, I'm thankful your father was the narcissistic asshole he was back then. If he'd been any more considerate, I'd probably be long dead and where would that put our pack?"

"Scattered to the four winds," Shawna whispered, clearly understanding. "I'll see about getting some refreshments for everyone."

"Thank you," Amanda said with a smile as she turned to talk with Demetri, Carly and Brandt.

Chapter Four

Sarina heard a commotion downstairs and went partway down the stairs to see what was happening. She saw Brody standing in the family room with her mother and a man whose back was to her.

"Look, I'm truly, very sorry about your wife's plight and her condition, but I can't allow you to stay here," said Brody.

"I under—" Brandt started to say before Amanda cut him off.

"You have no say," Amanda said to Brody, showing a true sign of leadership, a role she usually left to Romeo. "They are under my care and protection. Until I say otherwise, here is where they're staying."

"How can you say that, especially after what he did to Sarina?"

"I know exactly how you feel, Brody," Amanda said. "Do you think I love or care for her less because she's my daughter?"

"No," he snapped. Sarina grinned as he tried to reign in his temper. It was only part of what endeared him to her. "I need to clear this with Sarina, at least prepare her for it."

"I'm prepared enough," Sarina said, descending the rest of the way down the stairs. She walked over to Carly, running her hand along Brody's arm as she did so. She hoped it comforted him some as she understood his anger and the fear that fueled it. She gave the woman a hug and looked down at the twins who hovered around her legs. "They're adorable, Carly. Welcome."

"Thank you," Carly said, adding a small smile. Sarina noticed how frail Carly looked, especially now that she was so close to her time. Her middle was hugely swollen, evidence of the baby that grew in her womb. Sarina was thankful that her mother had the fortitude to bring Carly and her family to stay with them until she was once again strong enough to travel. Perhaps they'd eventually become part of the Delta pack. Taking a breath, Sarina looked up at Brandt now. He wasn't nearly as tall as Brody and his face showed the strain of the last few months. Somehow he'd aged what seemed like years, overnight. "You're welcome to stay here as long as you need." The surprise in his eyes made her smile as she touched his shoulder.

"Can I talk to you for a minute?" Sarina heard, noting the anger that Brody was feeling. She walked with him into the kitchen, far enough away that it'd give them some decent privacy.

"What the hell was that?" asked Brody.

"I'm inviting a woman who's obviously in need, to stay with her family, in my parents' home. Not that they really need my permission or anything, seeing as this is my *parents'* home. But I want them to know that they're welcomed here."

"While we're staying here… a man who seduced you under false pretenses?"

"Brody," Sarina said. "I understand that you're angry and I know that it's because you love me. I need you to know that I've made my peace with Brandt and I won't turn his wife away when she's obviously near her time. She's got two little ones and one on the way who need our help. I don't blame you for wanting to turn them out, but I won't do it."

"Then at least pack the boys up and we can go back to our own home."

"Our boys were taken from there once. I won't let it happen again. I just... I can't go back there until I know for sure that no one else is trying to harm us... not until I know that Lilith and Fenris are dead. I'm sorry."

"So you're going to willingly stay in the same house with that man?"

"No," she said, reminding herself to be calm, patient. "I'm going to stay in this home willingly with my mate and the children we made together."

"But—"

Sarina placed her finger over Brody's mouth before he could utter another word. "And Brandt and Carly will have their own space. Brody, I can't take your anger from you. I can only help you through it."

"Whatever." Brody's shoulders drooped as he relented.

Sarina sighed when her mate turned away and walked out the back door. She watched him pick up the volleyball, toss it in the air and spike it into the sand, spewing little crystals into the breeze. She didn't know what endeared him to her more, the tenderness he showed her, or the anger that often became her fierce protector. Maybe it was because all those hard-edged and soft emotions were all inside the same man, her man.

"He'll be alright." Sarina turned to see her mother and smiled. She drew her closer, wrapping her arms around her mother's waist. At fifty, Amanda Walker-Traverse was still a stunning woman. Sarina hoped to be just like her. "He just needs time to get his head around it all."

"I hope so," Sarina said with a sigh.

"So, where do we stand on wedding plans?" asked Amanda, taking the opportunity to change subjects.

"Not nearly as finished as I'd hoped we'd be. I feel like we've been doing this forever."

Coming around the long table, Sarina sat down at the kitchen bar with her mother. She poured over magazine articles and pictures for the next two hours before she stopped to rub her eyes. "Who knew planning the day I've dreamed of since I was a little girl would be so much work."

"Your father and I have been waiting for this day for a long time too. It's not every day you get to give your daughter away."

"Yeah, but maybe… maybe we shouldn't worry about all this fuss. We can have something simple out back, can't we?"

"You're the Delta alpha's eldest daughter, Sarina. Maybe if we'd done this before, things wouldn't have turned out the way they did."

"No," Sarina said, adamant. "I know that what happened, happened for a reason. Brandt was in a bad place, due in part to a bad leader. He wanted the fame and glory. He's not that same creature anymore."

"You'll have a hard time getting Brody to believe that."

"I know," Sarina said, looking once more out the windows that lined her parent's kitchen. Brody was still playing with the volleyball, but now he seemed to be working out instead of trying to pummel the poor ball as if it were Brandt's face. Kissing her mother's cheek, Sarina slipped off her stool and headed outside.

Brody knew she was there, despite not hearing the door open or close. She had that effect on him. Still, he didn't turn around and greet her. He wasn't sure he wanted to. His anger was still dangerously close to the surface and he didn't want it to boil over onto her. His pride was also deeply bruised, not that he'd readily admit it. He'd known Sarina was stubborn… there'd been enough signs along their journey to give him a rousing picture of her own temper. But for the life of him, he couldn't understand how she could be so nonchalant about Brandt staying in the same house as them.

"Are you going to ignore me all day?" asked Sarina.

The thought had crossed his mind, truth be told.

"I'm working on it," he said, finally turning to see her. She was dressed in a pair of old, ripped jeans, a baggy t-shirt and her hair was put up haphazardly in a ponytail. Still, Brody knew he'd never seen a more beautiful woman in the whole of his life. Letting the volleyball fall into the sand, Brody walked over to her. He grabbed her hands, running his fingers through hers. "I think I'd fail miserably if I tried to ignore you for even an hour. You'd just get pissed off and hit me in the head with something hard until I had to pay attention to you or risk unconsciousness."

"True," she said, chuckling. "I know this is hard for you to understand, harder yet to accept. I'm not asking you to be alright with them. I'm not even asking you to accept them and I certainly don't expect you to ask Brandt if he wants to sit down for a brandy. I also know I'd feel the same way if our roles were reversed. I just want to help Carly deliver her baby in an environment that's safe and secure. I want her to belong to a pack that won't pass her around from male to male until she's so used up that she's just a hollow shell of a person. For whatever reason, the universe brought her and Brandt together. Maybe because they're both a little rough around the edges. But they both have a chance to make something of their little family and I want to do what I can to help her, to help them."

Brody almost hated letting her talk. She always found a way to make him see things her way. "How do you always manage to do that to me?" he asked.

"Do what?"

"Make me see things the way you do, so that I'll give in."

"I get that particular gene from my mother," Sarina said with a smile and added a wink for good measure.

"Alright," he said, pulling her close and pressing his brow to hers. Tipping her chin up with his finger, Brody took her mouth in a gentle kiss. It still amazed him how deeply she could reach inside him. He'd never been great at letting people get close to him. Sarina had come along and thrown caution to the wind, not really caring what he thought or what walls he put up to keep her out. She just found a way over, around or under them. And if that didn't work, she grabbed a sledgehammer and knocked them down. It was true that he'd pursued her from the start, but it was she who'd done the capturing.

He'd meant for the kiss to soothe away the rough edges of his anger and smooth out her mood and the places where he'd hurt her. He smiled against her lips, knowing he should have known better where Sarina was concerned. The woman gave all of herself to whatever the task was. If it concerned the boys, she was all mother. If it was her parents, she was the dutiful daughter. When it came to making love, well, not that he was keeping tabs per se, but he had yet to find one fault with the way Sarina gave herself to him. She never held back, never asked for anything she wasn't willing to give in return. He'd known the moment he'd first laid eyes on her that she'd be his forever and it wasn't something he regretted.

Taking her hand, Brody led her inside, ignoring all the reasons they could both be distracted. Stopping at the base of the staircase that led to their rooms, he scooped Sarina up in his arms. He grinned when she giggled, but kept walking, ascending the stairs with her arms around his neck. "I'm not letting you go until I have you."

"I wasn't asking you to." Sarina smiled, pressing her lips to his neck. She reached down, helping him with the door to their private suite. Then he kicked the door closed behind them and shut out the entire world. Right now the only thing he knew, the only thing he wanted to know was how Sarina trembled when he touched her.

Chapter Five

Romeo sat with his main generals, sorely wishing he'd asked Brody to come with them. He knew his soon to be son-in-law needed to be with his family, to protect his daughter and their children, but Romeo sure could have used Brody's quick thinking tonight. "I need five of our best archers from each of your squads. We need to take out Fenris' scouts with quiet but extreme prejudice."

"What do we do once they're taken care of?"

"Then we attack the caves. There's only one entrance and exit from what I've seen of the inside. They'll have to come past us to get out. If we fan out once we get in, it'll be like picking off fish in a barrel."

"Can any of them turn?"

"I don't believe Fenris has that many wolves capable of being an alpha in his pack. He's not one to keep competition around. That means that most of the wolves are either betas or omegas. The omegas will want to dance around actual conflict so it'll be the betas that come at us first. Our alphas can make the change as we enter and deal quickly with the omegas. Then the rest of our pack can take down the betas. That'll leave us with Fenris and whoever the hell is helping him."

"Yes sir." The generals all agreed. The archers gathered with their bows and quivers filled with silver tipped arrows. Romeo supervised as one by one, Fenris' outer guards dropped dead. They fell from trees and hilltops that surrounded the caves, each one representing another break in the chain that Romeo knew had to go in order to keep his pack free and safe. If they failed, and failure wasn't an option, there wouldn't be a second chance to get it right.

"That's the last of them, sir."

"Excellent. We'll wait for day break to enter the caves. Let them start their slumber before we attack."

"Sir." Romeo turned to see his younger brother, Elijah, standing nearby.

"Eli," he said, "You're concerned?"

"I'd be remiss to not be at least slightly concerned, would I not?"

"Yes, but with you, it's often a natural state of being."

"I wasn't so bad before Penelope and Jeremiah. Now though, I see everything as a threat."

"I can't say I blame you. Maybe I should be a little more cynical."

"You're exactly as you should be, brother," Elijah said. "Leave the concern to me."

"Deal," Romeo agreed. "So what are you thinking?"

"I'm thinking that they're going to notice that their sentries aren't keeping watch anymore and that will wipe out our chances of a surprise attack. If even one wolf steps out tonight to get some air, we're in for it and without an advantage. Right now they likely know we're out here and are waiting for our attack as it is."

"You think the one who shot me knew it was me?"

"I think there's a damn good chance of it, yes."

Romeo had to admit the possibility of that chance was a good one. Clapping his brother on the shoulder, he said. "Thank you, Eli. We'll take measured precautions, but I think you're right. Listen up!"

Every man Romeo had with him turned to hear what he had to say. "Elijah, as always, has a valid point. We're not going to wait another minute. Their guards are down and I want this over. We attack just as it was discussed now."

Romeo nodded his head at his little brother and waited for Elijah to return to his own section before he gave the signals. Within minutes, they'd be fighting for their lives and the only thoughts on Romeo's mind were of his wife and children, their children and the legacy of the Delta pack. Amanda would lead in his stead if he didn't return home, but he kicked himself for not denoting Sarina and Brody as effective co-alphas should Amanda want to step down. Brody had been right in his argument that day. Sarina could and would make a determined, smart and fair leader. She was too much a mix of her parents to do anything less.

<<◇>>

"We need to go now, sir" said one of Fenris' lieutenants.

Fenris took a look at his pack, the ones who'd stay behind and knew that nothing would be the same again. Part of him was thrilled to finally have the upper hand on the Traverse clan, but a part of him mourned the world he'd known, the life he'd let die tonight.

"I'm coming," he growled, slipping out the back section and into the deep dark of the woods. As he fled to flank the Delta pack, the cries of death filled the air. He made his way with an entourage of betas and omegas through the woods, heading for the headquarters of the Traverse family. He knew the mansion well, had been there at least three times when Mabel Traverse had owned it. Then she'd purposefully harmed herself and he'd never gone back.

Flashback

"Fenris," Mabel said, grinning over her glass of brandy. "How are the caves this time of year?"

"Lovely. You'd know that for yourself if you ever cared to visit."

"You know that's not going to happen," Mabel said. She took a sip of her drink and sat it down near her bedside stand. "I won't give myself to any wolf, no matter how you or any of them try to persuade me differently."

37

"All because you love that human."

"No," she said, chuckling. "And the fact that you'd think that shows just how much you don't know about me, or them. Humans aren't our enemies. Most of them don't even realize that we exist. I won't give myself to a wolf from my pack or to any other because that's not why I'm here. I'm not here to satisfy some male's hormonal urges. I'm here to protect and provide for my family and our legacy. Anything beyond that doesn't concern me."

It wasn't the first time he'd come and Mabel knew it wouldn't be the last. After years of fending them off though, she grew weary of having to defend her reasons and her safety simply because they couldn't understand her stance. She'd lost track of how often they'd tried to scale the walls of her home, looking for the last Traverse woman to come into season. She hoped things would be different for her niece when her time came. She certainly didn't want her brother's child to deal with this overabundance of raging male wolves. And while she trusted Jeremiah and his kin to look after Amanda, Mabel knew that it was up to her to provide as much for her as she could. That started with the decision she'd finally come to over the night. It wasn't an easy one and never would it be something she took lightly. But her heart belonged to Stephen and as long as she remained the way she was, they'd never have a future together.

"Come right this way, Miss Mabel," Stephen said as he helped her into the downstairs bedroom. She was thankful now that she'd had the room converted. The

mere thought of walking up two flights of stairs to her personal quarters was a nightmare all on its own. "We'll get you settled and then I'll see about some soup."

"That sounds lovely, Stephen. Thank you."

"You're welcome Miss Mabel," he said. Mabel just smiled at him. Even now, he wouldn't admit to his feelings, although Mabel knew how they both felt. Stephen cared for her just as much as she did him. Her surgery was proof of that. She ate the butternut squash soup, enjoying the quiet of her home. Then she sank down into the comfortable mattress, pulled the thick down comforter over her shoulders and slept deep enough to aid her body in healing.

Four weeks later though, things went from turbulent to downright nasty when Fenris showed up with five very large alpha wolves. "Hello boys," Mabel said grinning. "Care for something to eat?"

"We're not here for food, Mabel."

"I figured that," she said, taking a bite of a juicy apple. "I hate to disappoint you gentlemen, but I don't have what you're looking for."

"Oh, I think you do," Fenris said, a low growl emphasizing his point.

"I don't, actually," Mabel said, looking him square in the eyes, a major moment of disrespect on her part. "I had my ovaries removed. I can't bear children, human or werewolf."

"What?" Fenris asked in disbelief. "You're saying that you're barren, that you can't carry a child?"

"I am, for all intents and purposes, as human as any other now. There's no benefit to trying to woo me anymore."

<<◇>>

"Sir?"

Fenris shook himself from the memory and followed the most seasoned of his betas further, deeper into Delta territory. As they neared the break in the woods that would lead to the Traverse mansion, a smile slowly crept across Fenris' face. Mabel had tried so damn hard to keep her niece, Amanda Traverse, safe. To ensure that she was wed, mated, and with child before any other pack could touch her. If only she could see him now. She may have disfigured herself, but Amanda and more importantly, her pretty daughters, were ripe for the picking. Sarina had already had two pups herself and Fenris knew, from good intel, that Amanda had one more daughter and a niece down the line. Fenris couldn't wait to see their stunned faces.

The mansion sat stoically in the open prairie, as if it ruled the land well on its own. Moving to flank the huge house, Fenris went straight to the front door while his betas took up posts on the sides and rear of the house. He stepped lightly up to the door and rapped sharply against the solid mahogany door. Making the change silently within seconds, Fenris didn't give the wolf who answered a chance to raise the alarm and ripped out his throat as he turned to face the doorway.

Within a minute he was inside, his betas following quickly behind.

They knew the drill. Amanda, Sarina, Gina, and Shawna were the priority. Getting all four women would be stellar, but he'd settle for whoever was home. Screams echoed off the walls as guards and innocent wolves alike were ripped apart. Fenris, the only alpha on this trip, stalked through the home of his greatest enemy, thoroughly enjoying the way his mark was being left.

"Did you hear that?" Sarina asked, sitting up in their bed. The sheet slid down, exposing her lovely breasts and Brody had to fight to pay attention to what she was saying. A week away from their wedding and Brody still couldn't get enough of her. They'd had a couple years together, had borne their sons, and still the need for her was overwhelming.

"What is it?" If it hadn't been for the look on her face, Brody might have tried to convince her that it was nothing.

"I don't know, but I don't like it," she said, already moving off the bed to get dressed. "We need to check on Gina and the boys."

"Alright," Brody said, pulling on his boxers. He scrambled into a t-shirt as Sarina opened the doors to their room. She headed for the room where her sons slept, thankful to see the two sentries still standing guard.

"How are they?"

"Still sleeping soundly, ma'am," one of the sentries said. She opened the door carefully and smiled when she saw her sons softly snoring in their cribs. She resisted the urge to gently stroke their soft, downy soft hair. Instead she thanked the guards again and met Brody at the landing that lead to the staircase. He let her lead, providing support as they descended the stairs. Then she saw the front door open and noticed the body lying in the entryway, torn to shreds. She skidded to a halt, feeling Brody's body stumbling into hers. She clamped a hand over her mouth as she turned into her mate's shoulder. His arms wrapped around her, holding her tight as she fought the need to retch. She hadn't known the wolf who'd stood guard at the front door well, but he was part of her pack and she'd grieve his loss later.

She took a quick moment to consider grabbing her sons and leaving with Brody, going into hiding where this evil wouldn't be able to follow. Then she heard Gina scream and Sarina's blood ran cold.

"Sarina Traverse!" a male voice called.

Sarina felt Brody's hands grip her arms tight.

"Come on, darling. You know by now that I have your young cousin. I'm guessing she's younger. She certainly doesn't smell like an alpha. Come to think of it, she doesn't smell like a beta or an omega either."

"She's human," Sarina said, taking a step into the walkway that lead to the kitchen. Gina sat with her arms behind her back, a large beta holding her captive. "She, for whatever reason, didn't pick up the werewolf genes."

"I don't believe you," Fenris said, grinning. "Sorry. It's sort of a habit with your family. You have a tendency to lie."

"I don't care what you believe, frankly. Gina was born three months early. Because of this, she never fully developed. She isn't able to breed and even if she was, she doesn't carry the gene for the change."

"Well isn't that a shame?" he said, turning to eye her cousin. "She's a pretty little thing. She would have made a great breeder."

"My parents won't let you get away with this, you know."

"Oh, right now I'm sure they have enough to worry about," Fenris said. "Although I can smell your mother nearby. She always was a bit elusive. Your father did well to keep her under lock and key until she'd borne his little bastards."

Sarina felt Brody grasp her arm. She willingly let him push her behind him. "What do you want, Fenris?" said Brody.

"Well, well," Fenris said, scoffing. "Finally coming to your girl's aid, are you? I'm surprised it took you so long. Word around town is that you're quite the hothead. Tell me you're not getting soft in your old age Duscene. She hasn't whipped you now, has she?"

"My mate knows her place," Brody growled. "As for you, you've more than worn out your welcome. Let Gina go and get the hell out of here before Romeo tears you limb from limb."

"I'm pretty sure Romeo is having quite the time trying to figure out where I am at the moment," he said, his eyes glacial and dark as onyx. "But we'll deal with him in due time. Right now, I'm here to deal with the women in his life. Now Gina here, she's going to go with Turk and enjoy getting to know the finer points of the male anatomy. Sarina, if you'd be so kind as to come with me, now."

Sarina watched as Turk yanked on Gina's arms, bending them up so that her shoulders strained to keep her arms in their sockets. She whimpered, her tears falling easily.

"Please," Sarina begged, taking a step toward him. "Please don't hurt her. I'll do whatever you want, but let Gina go."

"Sarina—"

She turned to meet Brody's dark, tumultuous eyes with her own calm ones.

"I need you to trust me now," she said to Brody, stepping into his arms. "Trust that I was born for this. It's my destiny now." She could see the war there, understood all too well why he struggled to let her go.

Chapter Six

Brody looked into the sexiest green eyes he'd ever known and knew he was either making history with this woman, or the biggest mistake of his life. He had to trust that she knew herself better than he did.

"Well?" he heard Fenris say. Only Sarina's hands on his arms kept him from ripping the alpha's throat out. He couldn't stop the low growl though. Seeing that it put a grin on her face was almost worth it.

"I love you, Brody Duscene," she said.

He pressed his brow to hers, wishing like everything that he could whisk her away, take her and their boys anywhere but here. Pulling her close so that her body pressed hard against his, Brody took her mouth, sliding his warm tongue past her open lips. Heat permeated him from the contact, warming all the cold places like only Sarina could do. Finally he tore himself away, mesmerized by the heat that still clung to him.

"Trust me," she whispered, a soft smile on her lips.

In that moment, he realized he did trust her and shame coated him for all the times he hadn't in the past. She wasn't just a beautiful, smart, capable woman. She was an alpha's daughter, born and bred to lead not just herself, but her entire pack if need be. Stepping back, Brody released her, biting his tongue so he wouldn't call her back and die trying to protect her.

He watched her walk toward Fenris and realized that white hot light started to emanate from her, like an overactive strobe light. Flashes that grew brighter and brighter until he couldn't see anything and was forced to shut his eyes tight and cover them with his hands to keep from going blind. Wind rushed past so that he fought to cover his ears and his eyes at the same time. It pulled at his clothes and nearly knocked him over with its power as Brody tried to remain standing. Forced to bend down on his knees, Brody dared to squint into that light and saw Sarina's bare feet mere moments before they disappeared.

Almost instantly everything was still again. Sarina and Fenris were nowhere to be found and from what Brody could see, neither were any of the betas or omegas he'd brought with them. *Trust her*, Brody thought to himself. Bolting into the kitchen, Brody saw no sign of Gina or the wolf Fenris had called Turk.

His next thought was to check on the boys and he ran upstairs, thankful to find them sleeping soundly still, the two guards outside the room still stood watch.

"Didn't you hear the shit going on downstairs?" asked Brody.

"We didn't hear anything sir," one sentry said, his eyes registering shock when Brody explained what happened. "No sir. There was nothing out of the ordinary up here."

Running a frustrated hand through his hair, Brody wanted to give into the anger and resentment. If Sarina were here, it'd be different. If she was here, he could crumple into a ball of instant relief. The fact that she wasn't required action on his part. But what action was needed fell outside his scope of comprehension and he only knew two people who could help him figure it out. "Where's Mrs. Traverse?"

"Sleeping, as far as we know, sir."

"I need her," he said. "I'm going to get Penelope Traverse. One of you guards this room at all times. The other needs to wake Amanda and have her gather whatever it is she needs to find Sarina and Gina."

"Yes, sir," the two guards said in unison. "But Penelope isn't at home sir. She went with Elijah and Mr. Traverse to hunt down Fenris."

"Then I'll wake Amanda myself."

"Where the hell are we?" Fenris growled. Sarina turned and smiled.

"Didn't you know I possess powers nearly as intense as my mother's?" Sarina chuckled at his apparent frustration. "You won't hurt anyone in my family again. Nor will you come within a thousand miles of the Delta territory. In this, you have absolutely no choice."

"The hell I don't," he fumed. When he went to strike her though, Sarina simply held up a hand and

47

Fenris hit a wall that none of them could see. "What is this mockery?"

"It isn't mockery, although I'm sad that I didn't use my powers before. I foolishly believed that you'd eventually tire of trying to end my family."

"Oh, I'll end you one by one if I have to. Turk!"

Sarina looked at the beta wolf who could do nothing but bow at her feet. This of course angered Fenris.

"You are no longer the alpha here," Sarina said, her green eyes glowing as light began to fill her from the inside out. "Fenris of the Holder Valley, you are hereby sentenced to banishment for your treatment of your pack. You will no longer be allowed within the borders of Holder Valley nor the New Delta region. As long as you stay outside these borders, you will be permitted to live. Break those barriers, however, and your life will end as quickly as it began."

"You can't banish me, you little bitch!" Fenris bellowed. Sarina's voice boomed now as if she held a megaphone to her lips.

"You have no say, Fenris!" she said, her voice making the once great alpha, tremble. "You will do as I command or I will see you ended!"

Only when Fenris bowed to her rule, did Sarina send him on his way with a careless flick of her wrist. His yell echoed in the darkened valley until it could no longer be heard.

"Sarina?" She turned to see her sweet cousin and immediately Sarina calmed herself, inviting Gina into the comfort of her embrace.

"Gina," she whispered. "I'm so glad you're safe."

"What about Turk?" asked Gina.

Sarina looked into Gina's eyes and grinned.

"Turk of the Holder Valley pack?"

"Yes, madam?" he said, not looking her in the eye.

"Stand please."

The large beta did as she asked and Sarina had a moment to wonder how he'd become a beta and not an alpha. Her only guess was that he wasn't the first born in his family. "You caused harm to my cousin and for that I am forced to punish you. However, I will reduce it to something bearable as you also protected her and went against your alpha to bow before me. Pledge your allegiance to the Delta pack and I will allow you to join our ranks."

"Sarina," Gina said, insistently enough that Sarina paused to look at her. Then she was in shock when Gina stepped back to stand beside Turk. When her hand slipped into his, Sarina couldn't keep the astonishment off her face.

"Gina," she stammered. "Can I talk to you for a second?"

When she stepped away from the strong beta and joined Sarina, Gina said, "Don't look at me like that." Gina face became radiant as a smile lit up her face. "I've waited my entire life, longer than you even, to find Turk."

"But he hurt you, Gina," Sarina said, feeling as if she was losing her grip on something precious. "You know I can't condone this. Your father, not to mention mine, would skin me alive."

"I just watched you banish an ages old alpha with a flick of your wrist. And you don't see what I see when I look at you."

"What?"

"An alpha. Jason was never meant to lead our pack," Gina said, her voice soft, remorseful. "He was meant to protect you so that you could lead us. I doubt even Uncle Romeo will be able to remain alpha when we return. You're stronger than even him now."

Sarina felt torn. Here was her grown, beautiful cousin asking for permission to be with a man who'd hurt her. A wolf who'd inevitably want to breed and she knew damn well Gina would never be able to give him that. "Gina, Turk will want a woman who can give him children. You know that's not a possibility for you."

"Who's to say that I can't breed?"

"The doctors who examined and took care of you when you were born?" Sarina said, feeling flustered. "They told your mom and dad that you'd never be able to bear children. Your reproductive organs never developed."

"Then how is it that I can stand here and tell you that I want him? I don't just want to be loved and cared for Sarina. I want him, my body wants him."

"Enough!" Sarina said. "I can't condone this, Gina. I won't condone it. That man hurt you and I won't give you to a man who'd harm you for his own sake."

"He didn't hurt me, Sarina. I only made it seem as if he did."

"I watched the tears fall from your eyes, Gina."

"And how many times have I done that in the past when we were kids to get you or Jason, or even Wade into trouble? You know damn well I can cry at the drop of a hat."

"I'm sorry, Gina. You'll have to take it up with my parents when we return."

"I don't have to do anything of the sort. I'm grown, nearly as old as you. I've nearly reached my breeding age and will decide for myself who I want to be with."

Sarina was at a loss there. Gina was old enough to decide for herself. Stepping back, Sarina said, "Fine. I can't stop you nor would I try to. You want to make a fool of yourself, be my guest."

Romeo swiped a frustrated hand over his face to wipe off some of the blood. They'd made quick work of the betas and omegas who'd stood against them, but there was no sign of Fenris and Romeo knew that the number of dead wasn't all the wolves from Fenris' pack, nor the pack that came to his aid. "We need to find Fenris!" he called over the echoes of dying wolves.

"Sir?" a beta called to Romeo. "You requested that we find Lilith's body?"

"Yes," he replied. Romeo followed the young wolf to a secluded room where a soft and decaying body lay. The stench was overwhelming and Romeo was thankful for once to not be in his wolf. He could only imagine how bad it would have been had he smelled her with his animal ability. "Take it outside and set it on fire."

"Yes, sir."

Romeo watched two of his most seasoned betas do as he requested. When the flames finally touched the corpse, Romeo could swear that it hissed at him. When the corpse was nothing but ashes, he asked Penelope to join him.

"What's up, boss?"

He grinned at her playfulness.

"Can you scatter these ashes to the four corners of the Earth?"

"Sure," she said, smiling. Lifting her arms Penelope called to her power. "To the winds of the north, south, east and west; hear my call, heed my request. Scatter these ashes to the ends of your regions. Keep them captive that they may never again build a body that will serve as a gateway for any evil spirit." As she spoke the winds picked up like a tornado, swirling around the fire and drawing the ashes of Lilith's rotting corpse far into the air. Within seconds the winds dispersed, taking Lilith's ashes with them.

Romeo grinned when she swiped her hands across each other as if she'd cleaned up a mess. In truth, he supposed she had. She was the only one who could keep Lilith's ashes from returning to themselves or finding another suitable host for her treacherous spirit. Even Amanda, as powerful and amazing as she was, couldn't do what Penelope was able to do. He supposed that's why the Radiants worked so well together. They had to depend on each other's strengths and admit their weaknesses in order to harness the collective influence of their powers.

"Alright everyone!" Romeo called. His pack gathered together just outside the entrance to the caves where Fenris' pack had once lived. "We need to burn the corpses of his pack and leave nothing behind. Once that's done, Penelope will cleanse this place."

It took nearly an entire day and night to rid the caves and surrounding area of all the dead from the packs that had sought to destroy Romeo's reign. Penelope spent that time gathering what she needed. She'd never done a cleansing rite without the other Radiants and it somehow felt odd to attempt something so great. "I wish Amanda and the others were with me."

"Can you do it solo?" Romeo asked, concerned.

"I should be able to perform the rite by myself, but that doesn't mean it wouldn't go smoother if I have the other Radiants here."

"I can call Amanda, see if she can come."

"I'd appreciate it."

It wasn't the first time Amanda had felt Romeo's call. It'd been nearly two hours since Brody had awoken her to tell her that Sarina had vanished with Gina, Fenris and one of his guards. She'd tried a locater spell that hadn't turned up the slightest bit of evidence and left with no other course of action, Amanda had been resigned to do as Brody was doing and trust that her daughter had things under control. After hearing Brody's account of what took place, she was almost positive that Sarina had come into her powers and she'd finally been able to relax.

Now though, she knew Romeo needed her. "Pen needs my help with a cleansing spell."

Amanda was busy packing what she needed when Brody found her. "Where are you going?"

"Penelope needs my help at the caves where Fenris used to be based. We need to cleanse them and the spell always works better when there's more than one of us."

"What should I do when Sarina returns?"

"Make sure that both she and Gina are alright. Then, help them rest. Shawna left a relaxation poultice in the fridge. You can split it between them and make them each lie down for a while. Should she need it, Sarina knows the room downstairs is always available to her, but whatever you do, don't let Gina go in there. She isn't strong enough to recognize the dream from the reality and could easily get stuck in her dreams forever. Her heart is too innocent."

"Alright," Brody said, agreeing to Amanda's instructions. He remembered the room vividly. He and Sarina had used it to heal the damage to their marriage once-upon-a-time.

Chapter Seven

Sarina came to in her own bed, thankful that she was back. Still, she needed to check on both Gina and Turk to make sure they'd made it back in one piece. As she neared Gina's room, she heard distinctly female giggles coming from the other side of the door. Not bothering to knock, she opened the locked door with a simple twist of her wrist. Stepping into the room, Sarina found her younger cousin sitting in her bed, laughing at Turk, who was pantomiming a flopping fish. A sigh of relief swept through her that Gina still had her clothes on and so did her would-be suitor.

"Hey cousin," Gina said smiling.

It hit Sarina then when she saw love, the deep and abiding kind in Gina's eyes. She looked at Turk and her heart felt both elation and apprehension when his own dark eyes seemed to mirror what she'd seen in Gina's. Her little cousin had fallen in love. Not with a human as they'd discussed, but with a werewolf. Sarina could only hope that Turk would understand Gina's condition, the limitations to her body's ability to bear children.

"Are you alright in here?" Sarina asked.

"I'm wonderful," said Gina with glee in her voice. "When do you think your mom and dad will be home? I'd like them to meet Turk."

"They'll be here shortly," Sarina said. "Mom just left a little while ago to help Aunt Penelope so we'll probably have a day to get through. But don't worry, they'll come home soon."

"Alright," Gina said with a grin. "Is it okay with you if Turk stays with me tonight? I'm a little afraid to sleep on my own."

Could she really stop her? Sarina thought to herself. She might be alpha material, but her cousin was a grown woman, capable of making her own decisions. Honesty had always worked before.

"I can't stop you from having Turk in your room, Gina. I'd caution you both, however, about your time together. I'd beg you both to take things slowly. I didn't and looking back, while the passion was wonderful, I might have enjoyed it more had I taken a little time to cherish it."

Turk stepped closer to Gina, reaching down to take her hand. "I'll take care of her, Sarina."

"See that you do, Turk." She turned with that and exited Gina's room before she said something she'd regret later. Her cousin wasn't a little girl anymore and she, like it or not, had no right to dictate to either of them what they could and couldn't do.

She headed downstairs, finding Brody laughing hysterically at Jedidiah and Brody Jr. who were desperately trying to toddle around. She couldn't believe how they'd grown. Much like in her womb, her little wolf cubs were eager to get on with living and she imagined it'd stay that way until they hit their fifth birthdays. She and Jason, to hear her mother tell it, were both eager growers and learners. Neither had slowed down to a normal pace until their fifth birthday rolled around. At nearly three feet tall, Jason had towered over her and had continued to do so until she hit puberty. She'd spiked in growth those first two years, meeting Jason on equal footing. Then he'd hit his pubescent years and skyrocketed past her, leveling out at an even six foot, two inches. Thinking of him still saddened her, but not like it had before, when it was fresh, the grief had been soul scorching. Now it was a dull ache that squeezed her heart, bruising it before relenting.

"These two are something else," Brody said, smiling at the boys. She had to smile as well. Ever since her sons had come into the world, they worked night and day to keep her and Brody on their toes. It wasn't just them either. When they'd been kidnapped, both Brody and Sarina had fought tirelessly with the aid of their family to bring them home safe again. Romeo had even offered himself to Lilith in exchange for his two grandsons.

"I still can't believe what Romeo did to get them back," Brody said after a moment of silence.

"I can," Sarina said. "He's always been that way, even as a dad. He never let us go anywhere or do anything that might jeopardize our well-being. He always prepared us for whatever consequences might result from our behavior."

"Still," Brody said, tousling Jedidiah's thick hair. "I can't imagine it was easy."

"No," Sarina said with a nod of her head in agreement. "I don't doubt it was difficult, especially trying to convince Lilith that he wanted her and not Mom. I imagine that was the most difficult part."

"You'd skin me alive if I ever kissed another woman."

"Yes I would," Sarina said with a chuckle. "And it's good that you know that. However, if it meant saving our children or grandchildren, I'd just carve the woman's eyes out and try to understand you only meant well."

"Uh-huh," Brody said with a sheepish grin. "Does that mean I can put my lips on Cassie Taite?"

"That skank from the butcher shop?"

"Oh come on," Brody said with a chuckle, treading on thin ice, but sure of his footing. "She's a cutie."

"If you happen to like STD's," Sarina scoffed.

"In that case, never mind," Brody said. "Seriously though, are you okay?"

Sarina looked up into Brody's eyes and smiled. He was the man she'd dreamed of as a young princess, hoping that one day when her time came, she'd know the love and joy that only Brody had brought to her life. Her love for her sons was just as fierce, but wholly different. While she loved them with her whole self and would die to protect them, her love for Brody somehow narrowly bordered on this side of insanity. Just a look from him could set her system on fire and it seemed as if it'd been forever since they'd been together. So much had happened, with Fenris showing up, banishing him, and dealing with Gina and Turk. She didn't know what to think or how to feel about anything. The last two years had been full of so much turmoil and love and life that Sarina was overwhelmed by all of it. Needing a few moments to herself, to quiet her mind and sooth her spirit, Sarina headed for the one place in her parents' home where she knew she could find peace.

"Welcome," a beautiful woman said. It wasn't the first time Sarina had seen her and she knew instinctively that it wouldn't be the last. The first time had been scary and intense, to say the least.

Thanks to this amazing woman, although Sarina wasn't at all sure that's what she was, she'd regained lost stolen memories, found the Brody she loved and now had a family she loved fiercely. She'd never let them go, no matter what the cost to herself.

"You're troubled," the woman said and Sarina was instantly drawn to her.

"I can't seem to concentrate on anything," Sarina said.

"Let's take a walk," said the woman.

Sarina took the woman's hand, gliding over new grass that tickled her toes. They walked and talked for what seemed like forever.

Finally the silence was broken when the woman asked, "Do you remember Lilith?"

Sarina couldn't help the shiver that ran down her spine. "How could I forget her? She kidnapped my sons, tried to make my father mate with her, basically turned my family's lives upside down. Am I supposed to forget her?"

"No," the woman said, a grin on her lips. "Of course not. Forgive me for assuming."

"Why do you ask?"

"Because she's made a special request that, unfortunately, her master has seen fit to fulfill."

"What's that?"

"She wants to take your place, Sarina."

"What do you mean, *take my place*?"

"She wants to swap places with you. She wants a chance to live your life."

"She can fuck off," Sarina said, the walls turning an angry black. "She had her time, twice if I remember correctly."

"It's not that simple," the woman said, sadness evident on her face.

"Why the hell not?"

"Because her master has levels of power here that nothing can refute. Not even my power can touch the support she has on her side. Her master now wants everyone in your home and the New Delta region. Somehow she's convinced him that she can get it from you. Even if you refuse, this will happen. Neither you nor I can stop it and struggling will only make it harder for you to return. I am forbidden to help you beyond this point, no matter your choice, but I can tell you that proving you are the real Sarina will not be easy, even for you. I beg you to accept this fate. Your powers, the abilities that lie within you are some of the strongest I've ever known of. Still, you'll need your reserves to come back from there."

"Would you be doing this if I hadn't come here?"

"Yes," the woman said regretfully. "I am bound to do his bidding regardless of how I feel about it personally. The good news is that you won't actually be going to his lair. He's agreed to let me keep you here, in this room, until you find your way home again. Remember though, Sarina, Lilith is as cunning and conniving as they come. She will have your family convinced within hours that she is you. Your proof better be damn good if you're going to refute her. Your powers may not be enough on their own. And, this room will take on a life of its own, as you well know. You will forget that this room was once a safe place. You'll forget that it can bend to your will. While you'll retain your powers, the longer you're in his grasp, the weaker you will become. Spend too long here and you'll find yourself trapped inside this prison, the one in your mind. Unlike our first meeting, you won't have a choice."

"Fine," Sarina said, feeling a wave of nausea sweep over her. "Let's just get on with it already."

Before Sarina could take her next breath the walls seemed to begin weeping dark, jet black, tar-looking sap. She knew there wouldn't be an escape here. The tar touched her toes and the more she tried to move, the quicker the sap climbed up her calves. It covered her thighs and hips, climbing slowly up her body until it covered her. Inhaling a deep breath, the tar slid over her mouth and nose, quickly covering the rest of her head.

With her eyes closed, Sarina sank down into what she could only describe as the pit of Hell. Screams pierced her hearing until she had to cover her ears with her hands and even that didn't keep them out. Her body writhed in pain as she sank lower and lower. Only when she stopped moving did Sarina dare open her eyes. Before her was a beautiful golden temple. She pushed the gate open, listening to the eerie way it creaked and groaned in protest. The beauty, however, was short lived. In a place this damned, nothing was beautiful.

Darkness covered everything, even what seemed visible. It permeated the smallest crack, never letting light or even the illusion of light to penetrate this sanctum.

"Welcome!" she heard, more in her head than with her ears. "Sarina Traverse, I can't tell you what a beautiful moment this is. I've wanted to make your acquaintance for a while now. I can't tell you how happy I was when one of my other tenants came up with a rather ingenious way to make that happen."

"If you're talking about Lilith, I'd caution you to watch that one closely. She is a bitch of the greatest proportion. I wouldn't put anything past her. Hell, she's probably scheming to dethrone you, no pun intended."

"Aren't you afraid to be here with me? I do have quite the taste for women with supernatural powers, you know. And I'm not too worried about Lilith. She's conniving and evil hearted for certain. But she doesn't have the rights and privileges I do. She can only go as far as my leash lets her."

"Why would I be afraid? You can cause me excruciating pain, but you can't kill me."

"Oh you're right about that, but I can make you wish I had."

Sarina saw his hand barely move before pain radiated along all the nerves in her body. Like an overpowered Taser gun, Sarina's body gave into the pain and crumpled to the floor, writhing as her body tried to fight the pain.

When he finally released her, Sarina was panting to control the trembling in her body.

"You tremble like that when your man touches you?"

"Screw you, you asshole!" Sarina said, anger seething through her. "You tear me from my family when all I wanted was a little peace. Then you sit there, cause me unspeakable pain and then have the nerve to say that?"

"I like to know about my prisoners," he said with a wide grin. "Not that it truly matters. I've been watching you since you were little. I know exactly what went on between the two of you."

"You're a sick f—"

"Aw come on now. Foul language is so last year. Not to mention I can make you forget everything you've ever known. If I so wish it, you'll be sucking my dick and grateful for the pleasure before you ever get your real life back. You wouldn't want to disappoint me now, would you? And I know you want that life back. So let's just calm down and get some facts straight." He paused to give Sarina a moment to reflect on his words. "First of all, you're in my domain now. What I say goes, without so much as a thought of argument. Secondly, be polite. Your mother raised a lady, so act like one. Now I'd like to hear it from your own mouth. How does it feel when Brody touches you? Especially that first time?"

Sarina knew that if she didn't want to have to endure untold pain and suffering, she had no choice now, but to indulge this demonic bastard. Sitting down to keep herself calm, she took a deep breath and told him about her first time with Brody, in crystal, lurid detail.

Chapter Eight

"You were a hot little number, weren't you? I certainly can't blame Duscene for mating with you. With that sort of sex going on I'm not at all surprised he fell for you."

Sarina clamped her mouth shut. A thousand retorts wound their way through her head, but she refused to give this man another moment's entertainment. She turned away and instantly found herself facing the fury of his anger.

"Don't you ever turn your back to me!" he growled. His hand didn't even move, but Sarina felt the sting of it across her cheek.

Furious that he'd even think to strike her, Sarina let white hot anger surge through her. She registered the shock in his eyes right before she blotted out everything around her in the white light of her own rage. When the light finally dimmed, she was someplace else entirely. She hadn't moved an inch, but whatever, wherever she'd been had changed completely.

"I thought you might like to see where you'll be staying for the considerable future."

"What'd she offer you?" Sarina asked, knowing he probably wouldn't answer her.

"Lilith?" he grinned. "Not much really. Although she did say something about specific members of your family. I considered it something comparable to letting her try one last time. She'll end up here eventually either way, so I didn't see the harm in giving her another chance."

Sarina closed her eyes, silently praying for Brody and her sons, her extended family.

"He doesn't hear you, you know." The laugh that emanated from him was hoarse and grated on her nerves. "I do of course, but then, I don't really give a rat's ass. All I want is for as many of you hybrids to make it down here as possible. Given your nature, it's likely you won't end up anywhere else in the end, but I'm not one for taking chances myself. I like a sure bet and you, for one, are as sure as they get, honey."

"So that's it, then?" she asked, her voice betraying her anger, resentment, and sheer hopelessness.

"I'd apologize for your plight, but I'm not really one for being particularly sorry." He grinned, slamming the door to a cell that would hold her prisoner until he wanted to let her go. It looked much like a prison cell with a solid, see-through wall on the front and the remaining walls were thick, solid, concrete. There was no toilet, no bed platform, just the walls that trapped her. She'd thought he was a dick before, but now she knew him for the purely evil bastard he was. She, like everyone she knew, had heard stories of the Devil.

Most of them were so far out there that she'd assumed they were made to scare little children into behaving. Now she knew better and she couldn't stop the shudder that ran through her.

"I'll leave you to your thoughts for now. They can be just as delicious as the rest of you."

Sarina watched him walk away, his laugh radiating pain along her nerves. She dropped to her knees, as much from the pain as the utter shock to her system. It was too much to take in, too much to adapt to. The woman had been wrong. Sarina didn't have what it took to dig out of this hole in Hell. Whatever pit she was in, there was no escape. Still, she wouldn't surrender. She wanted to scream, but was utterly afraid that he'd come back and torment her more. Did he know of her doubt? *Probably*, she scoffed. He seemed to know everything. Except, he'd made her tell him about her first time with Brody. Did that mean he hadn't known and needed the information? Or was he just testing her to see if she'd give it up? *Dammit!* Sarina slammed her fist on the floor. The resounding echo deafened her for a minute as light permeated her prison cell.

"Sarina!" She sat up straighter, Brody's voice resounding in her head. Standing up, she strained toward the sound. Barely breathing, she waited to hear his voice again.

"I'm here," she whispered, afraid her thoughts would give her away.

"Sarina?"

Yes! her mind screamed. Instantly, pain, excruciatingly unbearable rippled through her mind, short circuiting her connection to Brody.

"Didn't I tell you I knew your thoughts? Down here, darling, even the slightest neural change alerts me. There is no escaping here, sweetheart. There's no freedom when you're down here. I know your innermost thoughts and feelings."

"Then what was the point of your questions?" Sarina seethed.

"Simple humiliation. I find, even in your spiritual persona, you werewolves are extremely sentimental and much more like your human counterparts than you realize. Humiliation is a lovely weapon. It cuts deep without spilling a drop of blood."

"Screw you!" Sarina shouted, pounding her fist against the see-through wall. Light bounced back at her again, and Sarina noticed the barely perceptible moment of shock on the man's face. She would have called him the Devil, but somehow it wasn't a strong enough word to describe him. Concentrating her energy into light, Sarina let the light sweep through her until it vibrated along her nerves. Then she raised both hands and pounded the front of her cell, enjoying the sound of the wall shredding into a million pieces like a plate of tempered glass. She wouldn't have called it that, but whatever it was, it was breaking.

"How the hell are you doing that?" The astonishment in his voice was the best thing she'd heard beyond Brody's voice and gave Sarina the smallest sliver of hope. If she could surprise him, she could beat him and that was all she needed to know.

Brody woke with sweat pouring down his face. Reaching out, he felt Sarina next to him and he sighed in relief. He'd had the wickedest dream and still his body shook from it. Pulling Sarina closer, he nuzzled her neck, letting his hand roam over her body, reminding himself of the way her body swayed and dipped. In the three years they'd been married he'd made a study of her. He knew her contours well and loved every way her shape moved. Running his hand over her hip, he dipped down between her legs and grinned when she moaned, waking from her slumber. "I want you, babe."

"You're incorrigible," she said, smiling up at him. Her arms came around him, pulling him down to her. Using his lips, he ran warm kisses over her neck and shoulders, his hand moving up to cup her warm, supple breast.

"If you promise not to tell, I'll make it worth your while," he whispered, kissing her neck.

"What's your offer?"

"Morning sex and breakfast in bed?"

"Hmm," she mused. "I think that sounds fabulous."

He sank into her, reveling in the love they made. "I love you," Brody sighed as he leaned down to kiss her.

"And I you," she said against his lips. She kissed him back, her teeth grazing his full bottom lip.

"Ow!" Brody groaned, pulling back. Blood dripped from his finger as he touched a tender place where her teeth had cut him.

"Sorry," she said with a wicked smile. "I guess I got a little carried away."

"I'd say," Brody complained. He grabbed a wad of tissue from the bathroom and held it to his lip.

"I'm sorry," Sarina said. "I can make it up to you."

"Maybe later," Brody said with a sigh. "I'm going to go make breakfast."

After a shower, he let her rest while he headed downstairs and made omelets.

"You're up early," came a voice from the kitchen table.

"Your sister talked me into fixing her breakfast in bed." Brody grinned as he looked toward the kitchen table.

"She's a shark," said Jason with a laugh. "I don't even want to know what she promised you."

"That you don't."

Brody felt something stir the air around him, but didn't think much of it. In a house with a very powerful witch, something was usually stirring the air one way or another. It wasn't definitive proof that anything was wrong. In fact with spring coming, he was glad for the breeze. Sarina especially would enjoy the pretty flowers and fresh green grass. Maybe he'd plant some tiger lilies for her to enjoy, they were her favorite after all. Turning back to say something to Jason, Brody found himself alone. He shrugged, wondering where his mate's twin had run off to.

He carried the omelets back upstairs and smiled as he set a plate and a cup of coffee on the stand next to Sarina. "Breakfast is served, Madam."

She sat up, unashamed when the sheet fell down, exposing the peaks of her pretty breasts. Brody wanted her all over again. A flicker of memory slid through his mind and the woman in his bed shifted, blurring into a woman with jet black hair and eyes that were nearly as dark. He closed his eyes and took a deep breath. When he opened them, Sarina was smiling once again. He'd thought, long ago, when Lilith had been in his head that he wasn't worthy of the life he had. Sarina had stood by him even when he'd done deplorable things, irrevocable things. Now he was seeing Lilith in the woman he loved. Was that his punishment, to never be truly rid of that evil bitch?

"Jason seems to think I'm being swindled by you. You're a shark, he says."

"Does he?" she grinned. "Imagine that. What else does my little brother say?"

"Not much," Brody laughed. "Although he made it clear he doesn't want to know how I got talked into making you breakfast in bed."

"Oh please," Sarina scoffed. The sound grated on Brody's nerves. "It's not as if my dear twin hasn't had his share of bedmates. At least I stuck with my first one."

"Is that why you mated with me?" Brody asked, not sure where the note of anger was coming from. "Because I was your first?"

"What?" asked Sarina, a little bit surprised.

"You heard me," he demanded. "I asked if you mated with me because I was the first guy you f—"

"Would that have made it easier for you to leave?" Sarina said. "To believe that I mated with you because you deflowered me?"

"Oh hell," Brody huffed, running a hand through his hair. "I don't know. Why is it that every time things start to settle down between us, when we have a hope of peace; one of us has to stir the pot so shit starts all over again?"

"Maybe we're just better at conflict than its resolution," Sarina offered.

"Yeah," Brody said, offering back a smile that didn't reach his eyes.

"Wanna call a truce?" Sarina said with a sly smile on her face.

Something about the way she smiled tugged at memories in the back of Brody's mind, memories that felt stuck by some invisible force, making him unable to pull them forward for a good look. He couldn't bring them to his recollection, but Brody knew that something wasn't right. Pinpointing what was wrong though, wasn't remotely easy. "Sure," Brody said, agreeing with some trepidation.

Chapter Nine

Amanda and Penelope finally finished cleansing the caves and the massive outspread of Fenris' pack and the pack that had come to aid him. All but drained of their energy stores, Romeo had insisted that they stay and rejuvenate before anyone headed home. So, after three days and three long nights away from home, the Traverse clan and the Delta pack finally headed home. On the way back, Amanda told Romeo about the cabin in the woods, the one she couldn't see no matter what spell she used.

"That's definitely odd," he agreed.

"I just can't get past it," she said. "Shawna could see it and I know Sarina has seen it. But no matter what I did, it remains invisible to me. Something's not right about that."

"Have you looked through the journals to see if there's a clue there?"

"From what I could find, there's nothing about a cabin in the woods, especially one that's invisible."

"Well," Romeo said, being pragmatic. "We know that not all of your ancestors were great at keeping adequate information and actually documenting it. Maybe they didn't see the significance of it."

"Significant or not, I'm marking it in my journal. I don't want my grandsons wondering what's up with an ancient cabin in the woods, especially if they can't seem to see it. What happens when one of their mates stumbles upon it? I want to leave as much information behind as possible when my life ends."

"Sounds like a plan, but hopefully it won't be needed for a very long time," he said. Grabbing her hand, he pulled her closer. "You up to a little reunion when we get home?"

She laughed, giving him a small shove. "Men."

His own laughter rang out and finally the Traverse family felt the weight of war lift from their shoulders. Little did they know that not everything was wonderful back at the home front. Stepping onto their own private land, Romeo thanked his leaders and their squads, inviting everyone to a barbecue the following afternoon. Then he dismissed them to their own families and took his wife inside.

"Welcome home!" Sarina gushed.

Amanda embraced her oldest daughter. "Thank you, sweetheart." If she hadn't been so emotionally worn out, Amanda would have sworn there was something off about her daughter. Her hug was tight, but not personal. Sarina, the most mature of her children, had always had the most personal embrace. Maybe she was more exhausted than she'd realized.

"I think I'm going to skip dinner and get some much needed rest," Amanda said, begging forgiveness for her early exit.

"It's alright, Mom. I'll save you a plate."

Amanda slept fitfully that night and finally woke to the three-quarter moon as it shone high in the sky. Propelled from her bed, she found herself in the archives room leafing through journal after journal. Frustrated, she threw a journal at the wall and caught the movement of a board as it shifted just a hair. Moving the journals out of the way Amanda knelt in front of the loose board and pulled it aside. Sitting there behind the wall in the dust and cobwebs were three journals that looked as if they'd been buried behind the wall since the foundation was laid. Amanda pulled them out and coughed as she wiped the dust and debris off.

"Amanda?"

She heard Romeo call her name and answered him.

"I'm in here," she replied.

"What are you doing up this late?"

"I slept for a bit, but when I woke up, I couldn't go back to sleep. I had a bad dream that something isn't right here and I found a loose board in the wall, Romeo."

"Anything behind it? And what do you mean, something's not right?"

"Three journals," she said, holding the first one up. "They're all marked before the start of the first journal in our family's collection. I haven't started reading them yet. Did you notice that Sarina called me *'Mom'*? She never does that. It's always *'Mama'*."

"Maybe she's just worn out like the rest of us. Want me to stay and listen?"

"Maybe," Amanda said, feeling relieved for the extra company. "Still, it's not normal and it gets my brain overactive. I would enjoy the company." She waited for Romeo to sit down and get comfortable before she opened the first one to the front page.

June 1758

Headed down to the cabin tonight. It's one hell of a walk if you ask me. There's no mention of it from Father and Mother always defers me to him. She doesn't speak against him, but I can see it in her eyes. The doubt, the fear, the anger; she never says a word though. I used to think it was so noble and strong of her. Now I have to admit that I wonder if it's not just cowardice.

The cabin calls to me, in a strange, other worldly way. Like a drumbeat inside my head. Mavis and George can't see it and Mother won't tell me why. Why is it that I can see it, feel it even and they can't? I hope it means something good for them. I'd much rather it be bad for me than them. It frustrates them I know. They pester me constantly with questions, but I never indulge them. For them to know what I do is dangerous. They'll lead our pack some day and I can't have them wandering willy-nilly trying to spend time at the cabin when there's a pack to care for. If we want all of the New Delta area to be ours, we must maintain the strictest of protocols.

Christ. Now I sound like Father. He'd grin at that I'm sure. As the youngest of our family, perhaps it's my duty to protect this place, to keep its legacy for the generations that come after. Whatever the reasons, I'll figure out why this cabin is so special. It has to have some significance if it calls to me as it does.

September 1759

The cabin is relentless now in its pursuit of my time and attention. It's worse than a suitor coming to call each afternoon. Mother has voiced her concern, but I try to reassure her that I am simply enjoying the peace and quiet as I know I am quickly approaching my twenty-fourth birthday. Soon I will have no choice but to find a mate and become a breeder for our pack. I loathe to think about the idea, but I've already seen several of our men looking in my direction. I can't say I care for any of them one way or another, but Mother will insist on a match before long.

Still, the cabin calls and I answer as often as I can without raising suspicion. I don't feel any closer to knowing why this place stirs me as it does. The urgency seems stronger now though. Much more so than a year ago. Perhaps there's something for me to find or do before I reach the age when I'll mate. Either way, I hope to find some answers soon. It'd be nice to travel there for an actual reason. I have a hope that whatever this place needs to tell me, or show me, it does it sooner rather than later. Once I take a mate I won't be as free as I am now. There's no telling when I'll be able to come back.

"How far does this journal go?" Romeo asked.

Amanda thumbed through the pages, finding the last entry.

May 1760

Mother introduced me to Jameson Traverse today. Of all the suitors I've entertained, he's the most noble and humble of them. His dark eyes haunt me when we're not together. I have an ache for him that's new and exciting. He hasn't kissed me yet, but I dream of the day when he does. I haven't been to the cabin in nearly a month and the longer I stay away, the more it beckons to me. I have to admit that I've wondered what would happen if I didn't go back at all, but it seems even more persistent the longer I stay away. I wish I had more answers to put down. Maybe sharing my secret with Jameson will lead me to answers where the cabin is concerned. I'll go tonight and I'll take Jameson with me. I have to make him understand.

"We need to keep reading. Whatever this woman found or knew about the cabin, she put it in here," said Romeo.

Amanda couldn't have agreed more, but something was calling to her and it wasn't the journals.

"Do you hear that?" she asked, her pretty eyes full of concern.

"I don't hear anything," Romeo said. "But whatever it is you're hearing, keep listening."

Amanda followed the sound until she finally realized that it was inside her head. By the time she stopped, she was outside Brody and Sarina's room and the voice in her head was practically screaming. Amanda found herself knocking on the door, ignoring the telltale sounds of sex on the other side.

"What is it?" Brody obviously wasn't happy about the interruption, but a moment later, Sarina opened the door in a robe.

"Sorry about that," she said smiling.

Amanda looked at her and grinned. Then she looked into her eyes and everything in her froze.

"I'm the one who should apologize," Amanda said, forcing the words out. "I wasn't sure if you two had the boys. I didn't think to check their room."

"Oh, we haven't quite gotten to them yet," Sarina said, turning to eye Brody who still sat on the bed, the blanket thrown haphazardly across his lap.

"They were sleeping the last time I checked on them," he said, not quite meeting Amanda's eyes.

"Forgive me," Amanda said, her cheeks blushing. "I'll go see them in their room. Will you two be down for breakfast?"

"Probably," Sarina said. "I thought about making French toast."

"That sounds scrumptious," Amanda said with a smile. "I'll see you then."

Amanda headed toward the two guards that still remained outside the twins' room. "How are they?"

"Sleeping now, ma'am. They were up a little while ago and Carly played with them. If you don't mind my saying so, that's a woman who's about to deliver."

"I don't mind, I totally agree. It shouldn't be more than another day or two for her," Amanda said. "Keep an eye out, always. And try to keep Carly as comfortable as possible. Let Brandt know that if they need anything, it's at their disposal and Sarina's going to make breakfast in a little bit."

"Will do, my Queen," they both said before bowing. Amanda turned and made a beeline for Romeo.

"Hey," Romeo said, smiling. "Looks like you're on a war path."

"I don't know what to do, Romeo."

"What do you mean?" he said with a chuckle. "You always know what to do."

"Not this time," she said with a heavy sigh. "You'd believe me, right, if I said something that sounded insane?"

"Of course," he said, taking her hands. Amanda sought the comfort she found as his thumbs ran over the backs of her hands. Romeo was her anchor, the one person who could always keep her grounded.

"The woman in Brody's bed isn't our daughter," Amanda said in a rush, as if the truth was forcing its way out. "I don't know who she is, but she's not our baby."

"Amanda," Romeo said.

She knew the tone, the one that said without speaking, *take a moment to think about what you're saying*.

"I know it sounds crazy. You know I wouldn't bring this to you if I wasn't positive. I looked into her eyes and it wasn't our Sarina in there. Whoever she is, her heart is evil and she's using Sarina's body for whatever her intentions are."

"Alright," Romeo said. "What about our other children. Anything odd there?"

Amanda thought about her children and Jason's face came to her mind. She smiled, knowing he was out with a pretty girl tonight. Still, there was a void where he was concerned. She didn't know what it meant or why she felt such sadness when his face came to her mind. It was so soul-tearing that she eventually talked to Romeo about it. "I get sad when I think about Jason."

"It's hard when they grow up so fast, isn't it?"

"That's not what I'm talking about. It's deeper, darker than that. What if none of this is real?"

"What do you mean?"

"I mean, what if this moment, this life right here and now isn't our actual life?"

"You think because Sarina seems a bit off that what we remember is fake?"

"No I just… I'm just trying to figure out why Sarina isn't herself and why I feel such gut wrenching sadness when I think about Jason."

"Maybe Sarina knows. Have you confronted her about it?"

"No," Amanda admitted. "I don't think she'd tell me the truth, to be honest."

"Maybe we should both confront her," Romeo suggested.

"You'd do that with me?"

"Sure I would. If you think something's going on with her, I'm certainly not going to send you up there alone. You're my wife. It's my job to protect you."

Chapter Ten

Sarina stared at the legion of Hell hounds that growled and snapped at her, trying to figure out how she was going to survive, let alone escape. If he could read all of her thoughts, he knew exactly what to send at her. Her weaknesses lay bare before him, leaving little hope that she would ever return to the life she had, the people she loved. Suddenly a white door flashed in her mind and Sarina grinned. Meditation had been a phase during her late teen years and she'd become quite adept at blanking everything out so that only that white door existed. Sitting down, she began to chant, the white door looming large in her mind. One by one she put away her thoughts, compartmentalizing them so they could be taken care of when she was finally free. The more she put away, the calmer she became and even when she could hear her captor screaming in her ear, she still continued to focus on that white door.

Within an hour, Sarina felt the handle of that door and stepped through to freedom. At least that's what she hoped it was. Going from a white door into darkness wasn't exactly the most reassuring instance she'd ever imagined. Moving forward, Sarina saw lights in the distance and headed toward them. About an hour later she found herself on her parents' property and joy flooded through her. She was within reach of the porch when she saw Brody step out the front door. She raised her hand to call out to him when she nearly stumbled backwards. It was one thing to feel as if you'd been gone forever. It was something else altogether to come home and find that someone else was living your life.

Now Sarina knew some of what it must have been like for Brody, when he'd finally rid himself of Lilith's control of his mind. It must not have been easy trying to connect what he knew with what had really happened.

Falling back into the bushes, Sarina watched as her mate and whoever he was with walked along her parents' porch. Even with her excellent hearing she couldn't make out what they were saying. But her eyes saw when Brody pulled the woman close and kissed her. Sarina's heart twisted in her chest and she fought the urge to retch as she watched them.

Somehow someone was living her life and Sarina had no idea how to make everything right again. Who was mothering her children? She didn't even want to entertain the fact that this imposter was sleeping with her husband. Sarina tried to think back to when she'd first entered the room her mother had put in her childhood home. The more she tried though, the fuzzier her thoughts became. What had the woman said about Lilith? Was that who stood on the porch with Brody? Putting him in danger had never been part of her plan and now it seemed as if it might all fall apart. Taking a deep breath, Sarina straightened her shoulders with a resolve she was still trying to convince herself to have. There was only one path forward from here. She'd have to kill Lilith, again, and Sarina had grown so damn tired of killing and war. Words echoed in the recesses of her memory, fleeting across her mind as she tried to come to grips with this painful new twist in her life. She'd fought and clawed her way up from the depths of Hell, only to land right back in it again. Then a memory surged through her mind and she grabbed onto it, yanking it to the forefront of her mind so that she could formulate a plan to get her life back.

Brody wrapped his arms around Sarina's waist and pulled her closer. She came willingly and he grinned when her lips pressed easily against his. She didn't push or even ask for more, but the simple gesture moved him. There'd once been a time when he'd have simply turned her around, lifted her skirt and taken her quick and hard where they were standing.

Lately though, he'd found a liking for the slower, more methodical practice of romancing his wife. Well, she wasn't his wife yet, but with just days before their wedding, he didn't see the point in squabbling about titles. Sarina was his mate, the woman who'd captivated him from the moment he'd smelled her. From that first moment she'd gone full steam ahead. If only he could be that steadfast and confident.

"Your mind is running a mile a minute."

"Sorry," he said, grinning at her. "I guess I'm just trying to figure out how we ended up here. Things have been so insane and crazy since we first mated. I feel like I've lived six different lives since then. Has it really only been three years?"

"I know it can seem like a lot more with Fenris and Lilith and everything else."

"When the boys were kidnapped, I learned just how amazing and strong you are. I didn't give you enough credit before."

"And now?" Sarina said, smiling. "I learned how strong I was that night. Longest damn night of my life."

"Mine too," Brody said, nodding in agreement.

Brody kissed her then and they returned to the house, saying goodnight to everyone as they headed upstairs. "I'm going to check on the boys. Then I'll come and finish what I wanted to start outside on the porch," said Brody.

"Don't keep me waiting, baby."

Brody greeted the guards and stepped into the twins' room. He marveled at how well they slept. As newborns, he'd never have guessed they'd make it a night without waking. Now they consistently slept ten hours without so much as stirring to turn over. With no sign of slowing down, Brody knew sometime soon he would have to tell Sarina about his plans to prepare their house for toddlers.

"Brody."

He turned toward the sounds, grinning when Sarina stepped from the shadows.

"Are you that impatient now?"

"Brody listen," Sarina said, her serious voice getting his attention. "The woman you were kissing is still in the next room waiting for you."

"Nice try, babe," Brody said with a laugh. "I'm too tired for that sort of game tonight."

"I'm serious!" she said. There was a sense of urgency in her voice that caught Brody's full attention. He looked up into her eyes and nearly swallowed his tongue when moonlight poured into the room illuminating his wife's transparent appearance.

"Jesus. Sarina?" Brody tried to pull her close, only to realize his hand passed right through her. Studying her as if she were an alien life form, he stammered, "H-holy C-Christmas."

"Shh," she admonished. "We don't want to wake the babies and alert her to anything."

"How the hell are we going to deal with her and who the hell is she?" asked Brody.

"You're not going to bel—"

"I'll believe you," Brody said, meaning it. She smiled at him then, nodding.

"It's Lilith. I'm almost positive about it."

"And what the hell happened to you then?"

"I agreed to the terms of a contract I thought I had a good chance of fulfilling. She must have sold her soul to the Devil to get herself back up here and become *me*. From what I learned while I was down there, Lilith promised him that she'd get our entire family into his little human soul collector's edition. I tried to tell him that we weren't exactly human souls, but he wasn't buying it. He doesn't seem to care who ends up there as long as he can keep collecting people's spirits."

Brody grinned. It sounded just like his Sarina. "How do we get her out of your body?"

"That's the part I'm still working on."

Brody felt his gut tighten as they continued to talk. "How much did you see?"

"Enough," Sarina said, a sad smile on her face. "Bittersweet irony I suppose. The hell you went through I'm now going through and yeah, it sucks."

"Sarina I'm—"

"It's water under the bridge at this point," Sarina said. "I don't have the time to argue or be upset about it and even if I did, it won't solve our present problem, nor any other."

"So you want me to go back in there with her?"

"No," Sarina said. "But I'm not sure we have a choice."

"Sarina, she wants to sleep with me. Jesus, I almost—"

"Please," Sarina said, holding up her hand. "I know that it doesn't sit well with you. It doesn't exactly thrill me either, but I'm not asking because it's easy. I'm asking because it may be our last shot at finally killing that she-devil and sending her back to Hell for good."

"We need to warn your parents."

"Keeping her occupied is my best chance of finding my parents."

Brody sighed, running a hand through his hair. "Alright. But promise me you won't hold this against me."

"I can't exactly hold it against you when I'm asking you to do it," Sarina said, exasperated with him. "Now go, so I can finally get on with planning something to kill that whore."

Brody wanted to pull her close and claim her mouth in a hungry kiss that warmed her from the inside out. The struggle in his eyes told her then that he'd do as she asked, not because he was thrilled about the prospect of sleeping with Lilith, but because it'd help them save her family, people he'd come to care about just as deeply as she did.

Sarina watched him go, knowing he took a piece, the largest piece of her heart, with him. Then she slipped out the side door that joined the room on the opposite side and meandered downstairs. The house was quiet and by now Sarina figured her parents were in their room. She only hoped they'd listen the way Brody had.

Chapter Eleven

Sarina wound her way around the staircase, heading back toward their room when she heard their voices coming from the sitting room. It was her mother's favorite room in their home, one she was positive Aunt Mabel had loved as well. She turned and headed that way, enjoying the cadence of their voices. Then she stopped, just before she made her presence known. Tuning out their conversation, Sarina wondered if one more night of peace was too much to ask. Would they welcome her startling news or would they reject her? What if they couldn't hear her, couldn't see her the way Brody had? She was his mate, it made sense that they'd have that bond and connection. Would her parents have that same relationship now that she was a mated woman? Biting her bottom lip, Sarina turned once again, this time heading for the kitchen and the back yard. Sighing, Sarina knew she was going to ruin the peace that had falsely settled over their lives. She was both thankful for the time they'd had to enjoy it and cursed that she seemed to always be at the center of them losing it. She knew they needed to figure out a way to send Lilith to the depths of Hell, where she couldn't deal her way out, with extreme prejudice and as fast as possible, but she hated to be the one telling them about all of it. Sarina wished fleetingly that her powers allowed her to see the future, to choose the path that would most quickly lead to the life she wanted for all of her family. She would have saved Jason if that were the case. She would have spared Brody the torment of Lilith inside his head. She would turn back the clock and marry the man she loved, create a wonderful life and live it, knowing that Lilith and Fenris and their whole line was dust. Who knew one crazy bitch could torture a family for so long. Most people died once and it was all finished. Not Lilith. That female devil just kept getting back up.

Sarina went back to the sitting room that was now empty. Her parents had retired to their room. That didn't make her plight any easier. The last thing she wanted to do was walk into the middle of her parents making love to each other. She couldn't knock on the door so that option was out. She could hear her parents talking and wondered what their conversation was about. As a young girl she'd always been curious, sneaking around to hear as much information as possible. Jason would catch her and run to tell on her. That's when she'd learned to fight so she could punch him later for being a tattletale. God, she missed him. Not seeing him was like cutting off a limb. You always remembered what it was like to have it, even if it wasn't there to use anymore.

She knew what Jason would have done in this instance. He'd have found a way, without words, to make his point clear. But what would get her mother's attention? What would let her mother know that she was here and needed help? *Think Sarina.* She paced up and down the hallway from the kitchen to the front door and back again, unable to come up with anything she could use, anything she could do to make her presence known. An hour later, she was no closer to an answer than when she'd first started. Then, her little sister, Shawna came downstairs.

"Why the hell is it so cold in here?" she demanded, her voice booming as usual through the house. Shawna had always been the boisterous one, probably to keep up with Joshua, her twin. Those two fought like a mangy cat and a tempestuous dog.

"Shawna?" Amanda called as she stepped into the small walkway that led from her bedroom. Romeo was right on her heels.

"Maybe the air conditioning is messed up," said Amanda.

"I checked it, it's still on seventy-four," Shawna said, standing next to the thermostat."

Sarina watched as her father checked it as well. "Amanda?" he said, watching as his wife looked around.

"Shawna, was it cold upstairs?"

"No, just when I hit the bottom step and in here."

"Go toward the kitchen and tell me if it's cold there as well."

Sarina grinned when Shawna cursed as she hit the frigid cold in the kitchen. "Freezing," she yelled. "Son-of-a-bitch, it's cold in here!"

"Is the kitchen colder?" Amanda asked, following her suspicions.

"About the same," Shawna said, her teeth starting to chatter. When she headed back toward them, she was rubbing her arms to warm them. "What's going on?"

"What are you thinking?" Romeo asked, eyeing his wife. He grabbed his jacket off a hook by the front door and draped it over Shawna's shoulders.

"Thanks, Dad."

"I'm thinking our girl is trying to reach out the only way she knows how," said Amanda.

"By freezing us to death? And who are you talking about?" Shawna asked, her lips still moving.

Amanda gestured for Shawna to lower her voice. With Romeo beside her, Amanda was able to explain her suspicions about Sarina to Shawna. After a brief moment to absorb the shock of the news, Shawna nodded her acceptance of the situation.

"So what happens now?" asked Shawna.

"When Sarina and Jason were little, they would play all the time, but Sarina was always the practical one. She followed the rules, did what was asked of her. Jason was the innovative one. Sarina needs to talk to us, but if my suspicions are correct, she can't do it the way we are now," said Amanda.

"Still doesn't tell me why we're freezing," said Shawna.

"She paced up and down here," Amanda said, following the path Sarina walked. "The more she did so, the colder it got. Unfortunately I don't think she's here now. It's no longer cold here and it's not getting colder anywhere else. When she comes back, I'll be ready to find her. Meanwhile, you keep an open mind. If your sister is trying to communicate with us, it means whoever is up there with Brody isn't our Sarina. Be careful."

"I will be," Shawna said. When her parents had gone back to their room, Shawna hung her father's coat back on the hook and headed upstairs. Checking in on her nephews, she smiled when she saw them sitting up in their beds. "Well hello there handsome." Shawn picked up each boy, pressing a kiss to their downy hair.

"Beautiful aren't they?" Turning, Shawna stared at her sister. Sarina was resplendent, obviously glowing as she pulled on a robe.

"That they are," Shawna said, careful not to let her alarm show.

"So, I thought maybe later we could go over some wedding plans? I don't want my maid-of-honor-to-be out of the loop."

"Sure," she said, putting on her best fake smile. "I'd like that."

"Great," Sarina said, smiling back. "I'm going to get back to Brody if you still want to play with them."

"Sure," Shawna said again. "I'll watch them for a while."

"Great, thanks."

"No problem, sis." Shawna sighed heavily when Sarina went back to her room where Brody was. Shawna stayed with her nephews for some time before she left. She tried not to think about Brody with whoever had taken over her sister's body. Still, what could any of them do? She couldn't just come out and warn Brody about the woman he was sleeping with. *Talk about sleeping with the enemy*, Shawna thought.

Descending the stairs, she turned toward the kitchen and nearly screamed before she clamped a hand over her mouth. "Holy Jesus," she whispered. "What are you doing here?"

"Nice to see you too, little sister."

"I thought you were off on your honeymoon?"

"I wish," Jason said with a smile. "I actually stopped by because Sarina needs my help. Is she here?"

"Um, no," Shawna said, nervously. "I haven't seen her. She's indisposed at the moment."

"I bet she is," Jason said, grinning. "But I'm not talking about the woman who's up there with Brody. I'm talking about the woman who made it the Arctic Circle in here just a bit ago."

"You know about that?"

"I know about everything, baby sister, and that's nothing."

"Do tell, big brother," said Shawna with a chuckle.

"You wouldn't believe the half of it, sweetheart. But suffice it to say that this," he moved in a circle with his hands extended, "this reality, as you know it, isn't quite what it seems. Everything's in the right place and all, but there's someone here who shouldn't be. Our sister needs our help to get her back where she belongs and to keep her here."

"And how am I supposed to do that? According to Mom, all I'm good for is waiting to turn twenty-four so I can take a mate."

"She sees more in you than that, Shawna," Jason said, his dark eyes going soft and sad for a minute. "She just has a lot on her plate with Sarina right now and rightfully so. Our sister needs to have her life settled down some. Try not to hold it against her."

"Figures you'd stick up for her," Shawna said with a pout.

"I'm not sticking up for anyone. But I do have important information that will help our Sarina find her place and get rid of the being who's trying to take her place."

"I miss you, big brother," Shawna said chuckling as they headed toward the kitchen. "Help me finish off the cookies in the fridge so I don't eat them all."

"Deal," Jason said with a smile. "So tell me about this Demetri Benikov."

"He's nothing, just a wolf who's interested in me."

"Mom and Dad are hardly going to see that as nothing."

"Mom already knows some of it, but I couldn't bring myself to tell her the whole truth."

"Why? She's always been able to listen to us without judgement."

"Because I'm not even sure what it means. I… I love him. I love that he's respectful of me and our pack. I love that he's smart and quiet and peaceful. I love that when you push him, he'll dig his heels in and stand for what he believes is right, no matter who's challenging him."

"Well, he sounds great," Jason said. "But I'm not sure I'd want him challenging Dad. Although Dad is rarely affected by anyone speaking their mind. It's good that Demetri can do that. You'll need a man who can stand up for you, protect you."

"I want to be with him and that is the crux of the problem."

"How so?"

"Because," Shawna said, irritated that she needed to explain herself. "As a breeder, I'm supposed to be a virgin on my twenty-fourth birthday. Even if I chose not to be, I wouldn't come into heat until then. My big question is, what happens if I'm not? What happens to me if I choose to give myself to him?"

"Well, I obviously am not going to tell you what to do. That's a decision only you can make. I will say, however, that if Demetri loves you, he'll support whatever decision you make. If you want to be with him, little sister, I say make every moment count. I often wish I had done the same. And remember, when you wake up tomorrow morning, Demetri needs to know how you feel."

"Alright," Shawna said as she sat two more cookies in front of Jason.

Shawna ate her cookies with her brother, enjoying his company more than she could ever remember. He'd always been overbearing, always telling her what to do, what not to do. Now he seemed so relaxed, as if everything would just work itself out.

Chapter Twelve

After her chat with Jason when Shawna crawled into bed, she fell asleep with a smile on her face. The smile didn't last long as Shawna woke the next morning and almost died of a heart attack, her heart was beating so fast. The memories of her dream were still fresh in her mind as she crept quietly toward Jason's room. Cracking open the door, she felt the flood of tears overwhelm her as she remembered that her big brother was dead. Dead because a she-bitch of a werewolf had killed him. Sick to her stomach, Shawna let the tears come for nearly half an hour before she could stop crying. She grinned at the picture of their family on Jason's desk. Picking it up, she held it lightly. "Thank you, big brother," she whispered. Turning, she quietly closed his door, leaving behind the past.

"You look chipper this morning," Joshua said when she entered the kitchen. She grabbed a biscuit, scooped up some of the scrambled eggs he'd made and grabbed two pieces of bacon.

"Thanks," she said with a grin.

"No problem," he said, pouring her a glass of orange juice as well. Amanda had taught her children that there wasn't men's work or women's work. Work was always there and she'd taught her five children to cook and clean up the mess afterward. Laundry, dishes, bathrooms were all chores she'd taught them to do. Oftentimes as they were growing up, she'd put them in pairs, especially if they were quarreling. "So why the good mood?"

"I'm going to propose to Demetri Benikov today," Shawna said.

"W-what?" Joshua said with a stutter. "Do Mom and Dad know about this?"

"No," she said with a chuckle. "I'm not proposing. I'm just going to tell him that I have feelings for him."

"You might want to wait until he tells you something similar. Men don't like to feel pressured."

"Pressured my ass," she scoffed. "He drools over me whenever we're within eyesight of each other."

"And I take it you feel about the same way?"

"I've wanted him for a while now," she said, laughing when he looked very uncomfortable. "But don't worry. I won't bore you with the details."

"Thank God," Joshua said, feeling relieved and laughing. "I'll pay you the same courtesy about Cassie Sorenson."

"Oh, I like her. Good choice, little brother."

"Little my ass," Joshua goaded her. Younger by a mere few minutes, Joshua hated being the younger of the two last Traverse children. "I'll be bigger than you forever, little sister, and when we're old, I'll be younger."

"True," she said. "I suppose we're even then."

"Damn right. Tell Demetri I said *'hey'*. Maybe I'll see if he wants to hangout sometime."

"I'm sure he'd like that," Shawna said. She didn't mention that depending on how things went when she told Demetri how she felt, there either would or wouldn't be an invitation to hang out with Joshua. Shawna certainly hoped to extend the message from her brother in person.

Amanda saw her youngest daughter in the kitchen and headed that way. "You're heading out?" Amanda asked.

"Yeah," Shawna said with a bright smile. "I got some much needed encouragement to seize the day."

"Oh?"

"I saw Jason in a dream. He told me not to waste another minute. Life is short."

"That it is," Amanda agreed. Stopping her daughter, Amanda pulled her into a hug. "Be careful. And practical. I know that's more Sarina's area of expertise, but I'm just saying."

"I know," Shawna said. "I should be back just after lunch."

Amanda watched her daughter leave and sighed. Three short years and all of her children would be where they were meant to be in the Delta pack. They'd start grooming Sarina and Brody for becoming the alpha couple and Amanda would hopefully, finally be able to enjoy being a grandmother. She headed up to see Jedidiah and Brody Jr., passing their parents' room as she headed over to the twins' room. *Come home again, darling*, Amanda thought as glanced at their door. She knew the Sarina who slept in the adjoining room wasn't her daughter, but how to prove it without letting whoever that woman was know it?

"Gramma," Brody Jr. said, extending his arms. Amanda spent an easy and blissful morning with her grandsons before she tucked them in for a nap and tiptoed out. She checked on Brandt and Carly to see how they were fairing with their twins. Then she headed downstairs to have a discussion with a particular woman.

"Your highness," the beautiful woman said. But Amanda could see the tortured look in her eyes.

"I've come across some troubling occurrences of late and I'm afraid I need some clarification."

"Yes, madam?"

"Sarina, is she dead?"

"No," the woman answered immediately. "Not dead, but definitely in need of assistance."

Amanda watched the woman carefully inside her private shelter. The room had always been meant to heal, to help those who needed its assistance. Amanda wasn't sure if that was still true. The woman, someone Amanda had always considered a friend, was clearly in pain and the more she talked, the worse it became.

"Tell me what you know," Amanda demanded.

"I sent her down to Hell inside this place because the one who controls me demanded it of me," the woman cried as her body writhed under obvious duress. "Lilith convinced him to free her soul in exchange for Sarina and a hope of snagging your entire family."

A storm of white hot anger bubbled inside of Amanda as she thought about what Sarina had gone through. The colorful walls that so often picked up hues of a person's feelings where startlingly white, nearly blinding in its intensity as Amanda raged around the room. Her powers, safe to express inside this place came in full force. She created hills and valley, lush with trees and all types of flora, only to destroy them again with an earthquake that would have devastated anyone living in her creation. Sometime after she'd first entered the room, Amanda walked back out and closed the door. Drained from the use of her powers, she climbed the stairs to her room and sank onto the bed. Without so much as a greeting or explanation to anyone, she shut out everything and everyone, because when Sarina came back, Amanda would be ready.

-To be continued in Book 5-

If you enjoyed this title, I would appreciate your leaving a review of the book. Good reviews encourage an author to write as well as help books to sell. Good reviews can be just a few short sentences describing what you liked about the book without having a spoiler. If you could spend 30 seconds writing a review, I would appreciate it: you can review this title right now at your favorite retailer.

Here is a preview of the **next story** you may enjoy:

Alpha Revelation: Romeo Alpha Blood Lines Romance, Book 5

"**WE'VE GOT** some serious decisions to make," Amanda said, chuckling when Romeo rolled his eyes. Deep down, she felt uneasy proceeding with the wedding while everything was still in turmoil but for now, she had to play along. "Well, it's not every day you give away our eldest daughter you know."

"Seems to me I did that a while back when she mated that little whelp," said Romeo, joking.

"Oh come on, he's good for her."

"Meh," Romeo said, with a careless shrug of his shoulders. "He's alright."

"You love him and you know it." Amanda smiled.

"Yeah well, I can't hate him forever. Sarina would never talk to me again."

Amanda rolled her eyes and slid her arm through his. She loved him, even if he was twice as stubborn as any man she'd ever met, human or not. Had it really been nearly twenty-eight years since he'd all but forced her to marry him? Okay, he'd been nearly irresistible, but still; he'd also been an annoyingly arrogant dick. "Would you have picked anyone different?"

He turned those smoky eyes on her and set her insides fluttering with his crooked grin. "Honestly? Never. I wasn't about to tell her that. But Brody fits her to a T and…," he paused with a sigh, "you were right."

"Excuse me?"

"When you said she'd hate us; that we'd destroy any trust she had in us. You were right."

Amanda smiled, but not laughingly. It had certainly been a tense moment in their family.

If only she'd known then how much more tense things would get from that moment on, perhaps she'd have been somewhat prepared. The last three years had been both joyous and torturously painful. She'd welcomed two healthy, bouncing grandsons into their pack, thanks to Sarina and Brody. She'd also buried her eldest son, Sarina's twin, Jason. She'd fallen apart and somehow put herself back together after his death. Now, things started to settle down. That is, until last night when she visited the special room and spoke to the beautiful keeper of that room. Amanda sought her council after suddenly feeling the weight of worry that Sarina was not actually *her* Sarina. The bond between mother and child is one of the strongest and purest in nature, and when she went to hug Sarina earlier that evening, she felt something missing. A feeling of warmth and sincerity that was non-existent.

Faced with terrifying knowledge that Lilith had managed to convince the Devil himself to allow for her to inhabit Sarina's body, and therefore also aiding in the eventual destruction of the entire Traverse family, Amanda had no time to waste. Torn between saving her daughter or ruining a joyous occasion her family was looking forward to, the latter would have to wait. Of course it could wait! Her daughter was being held captive in purgatory! Giving her head a shake, she wrung her hands as a worried look furrowed her brow. She decided to broach the subject with Romeo with the most delicate touch, so as not to anger him beyond control, especially when he finds out that Lilith is behind it all. She couldn't risk Lilith using her incredible power to keep Sarina a prisoner forever, or worse, end her daughter's life altogether. Lilith could be unpredictable and extremely dangerous if she knew Amanda and Romeo were on to her, especially before Amanda was prepared with a plan to save their daughter.

"You're brooding again," Romeo said as he drew her into their room. "Not that I don't find it incredibly sexy."

Amanda giggled when his lips found the nape of her neck and his arms came around her waist.

"Your mind is so sexy when you're brooding. Wanna do some brooding in the buff?" he asked.

"And you're incorrigible. But you did get me to stop brooding, for a minute."

"If the promise of sex keeps you from sulking, I can make good on it," Romeo said teasing, playfully nipping her shoulder.

Amanda sighed, wishing that an afternoon romp would cure all her worries. "I just… ever since we got back from defeating Fenris, I just can't shake the feeling that something's not right. I haven't said anything before now, because I wanted desperately to deny it. Now though, that feeling's getting stronger almost by the minute."

"Have you done any spells to expel it?"

"No," Amanda said, not sure she could explain why. She knew she had to try though, for everyone's sake. "I know this sounds crazy, I've almost convinced myself that it is, except I know in *here* it's not." She placed her hand over her heart.

"Well?" Romeo urged.

"I think there's something wrong with Sarina."

"But you don't know what?"

"Right," Amanda sighed, even though she knew this was not entirely true.

"Maybe we can work together to narrow down what the difference is. I don't suppose we could chalk it up to her excitement about the wedding?"

"No and that's just it. She doesn't seem excited. Two weeks ago she appeared ready to just get on with it. I figured after nearly three years together, maybe it was just a formality to her. But then, as everything settled down she was beaming about it. Now we're back to *'I couldn't give a shit.'*"

Amanda knew pretty much what he was thinking when she looked at Romeo. She didn't need telepathic abilities to know what was on his mind.

"Maybe we've all been a little too relaxed," he finally said, his dark eyes meeting hers.

"You think something's wrong as well." It wasn't a question, but a statement of undeniable fact.

"I think you're not the only one who's noticed changes," he agreed.

"Why didn't you say anything?"

"Because she already thinks I'm paranoid. I wasn't sure what I saw was real or if it was just a figment of my imagination."

"So what do we do?"

"What else? We confront her with something she wouldn't know unless she was our Sarina."

"Such as?"

"What it was like when she was with Brody that first time," Romeo said, refusing to flush at the idea of his daughter being with a man. "Only our Sarina would know the answers to those sorts of questions."

"You want to question whoever is pretending to be our Sarina with intimate questions about her first time. Any woman can answer those questions." Amanda balked at this suggestion.

"Not the way our daughter can," Romeo said, grinning when Amanda sighed.

"Have fun with that one," Amanda said in retort, now sporting her own wide grin.

"Oh no," he started, putting both of his hands out, palms facing her. "I didn't say *I* was going to talk to her, I said *we* should. You know damn well I'm talking about *you*, woman."

Amanda's laugh poured out so naturally that Sarina felt tears sting her eyes. She might not have had the body she once did, but her emotions were still her own and they were heightened, especially given the circumstances. How do you convince your mother that you were real and not a figment of her imagination when she can't hear you? Brody had believed her, but he'd been able to hear her, even to see her somewhat. Telepathy, through mates, was a natural part of being a werewolf. She just hoped her mother could hear her as well. There was hope, knowing that her mother was a Radiant. It wasn't the first time she'd been able to hear someone she loved, despite great obstacles.

Sarina remembered her mother telling her that when she'd been pregnant with Sarina and Jason, Amanda had been tucked safely inside the in-between realm in Ireland. Even then, she'd been able to step outside that space to hear Romeo. It had held her together over the months of their separation when he'd been held prisoner by her Aunt Aurora's obsessive ex, Remus.

That time seemed like forever ago and Sarina felt her heart drop again when she thought about her now deceased brother. The mere fact that she hadn't seen him in the underworld was cause for celebration, but her heart wasn't in it yet. She needed to get her life back and her mother was her only hope of doing so.

If you enjoyed this sample then look for **Alpha Revelation: Romeo Alpha Blood Lines Romance, Book 5**.

Here is a preview of **another story** you may also enjoy:

Romeo Alpha: A BBW Paranormal Shifter Romance - Book 4

AMANDA FELT like she had just been hit by a ton of bricks. Her husband Romeo and his twin brother Damon had been on the outs because of Elena, the witch who had tried to use dark magic to lure Romeo to her. Elena had torn Romeo's family apart and was supposed to be dead by Romeo's hand. Yet here she was, standing in front of them.

"I thought I killed you," Romeo said sternly, narrowing his eyes at Elena.

Amanda couldn't help but notice that the woman was incredibly beautiful; thin like a super model with long, flowing hair the color of redwood. But there was also something about her that reminded Amanda of a cat. Her movements and eyes looked feline.

"You almost did, but I'm pretty resilient. Sorry about my companion's behavior." Her words came out airy and wispy like her voice was being carried on the wind a long way. "Harming you, kidnapping you, was never my intention."

Elena approached Remus' body, and Audri glared up at her, encircling him with her arms for protection. Elena ran her fingers over his cold cheek and stood back up straight. "What a shame. I'm afraid either side he was on would have been a losing one for him. Dean never has been very forgiving. Well, I can see I've kept you a while, and I know you must be dying to get back to your little cubs."

Amanda gripped Romeo's arm so hard she felt she might break his bones. "What do you know of them?" she asked through gritted teeth. She was ready with her power, waiting for the moment to strike. She didn't like the way Elena had miraculously come back to life, how she had sucked the power from a dead man, or how she was looking at all of them like prey now.

"No need to fear me. I can simply feel that you have given birth recently. And since I don't see the little ones, I would assume that they are hidden somewhere safe. That was very smart of you. Dean surely would have used them against you."

Amanda was sure she heard a threat hidden under that statement, but she said nothing. She was ready to go home.

"I'll be seeing you." Elena turned and walked away slowly, leaving all of them in shock.

"Amanda?" Penelope stepped forward to embrace her.

Amanda suddenly felt something in herself let go, and she began to cry. They were reunited, finally, all of the Radiants and their daughters.

"I'm so glad you're all right," she whispered through tears as the rest of the Radiants stepped forward.

"Amanda, I must stay behind for a while and let my family see that I am all right. I will be to your home soon to continue our training. Would you mind taking my daughter with you? I will send Alessandra with you as well." Catrona looked at her with a soft smile. Even after being trapped in a crystal for months, she still exuded so much confidence and beauty.

"It would be my honor," Amanda replied, taking Catrona's daughter's hand. Amanda closed her eyes and felt the power running through her. Her time with Ariella had made sure that she knew all there was to know, perhaps even more than Penelope did, about being a Radiant. She couldn't wait to tell Penelope all about her time in Faerie.

She felt the Earth and the ley lines, all the energy the Earth provided her, and she willed all of them home.

<<◇>>

November 7, 2014

I am happy to say that Romeo and I are finally back at the estate for good. The repairs are all finished, and though we lost much of the furniture and the downstairs, the library room with the diaries, and my bedroom are miraculously still intact. Sometimes, I think there must be someone watching over me. I'd like to think it's my parents or maybe even my aunt. I reread her diary from time to time and talk with others about what she was like. I see more and more of her in myself each passing day. She was such a strong and loving woman. I wish I could have known her.

As far as Elena, or Lilith, or whatever the witch's name is, everything has been rather quiet on that front.

117

It may be the calm before the storm, but I have enjoyed the time of peace to spend time with my new husband and my two beautiful children. They look like the perfect mix of both Romeo and I, and I am so proud. They are already learning to sit up and are cooing and laughing. It brings more joy to my life than I ever could have imagined.

However, there are other issues to address. Today is going to be a big day. The Radiants are having a meeting to decide whether or not they should all stay here any longer. Our powers are starting to cause many disturbances in the weather and the environment, just like they warned me it would. But I still feel uneasy with them going. I can feel something brewing, and it's coming soon. Hopefully, I can keep them from leaving just a little while longer.

Tonight, we are also holding a formal ceremony to honor both Damon's and Remus' life. Not everyone agrees with it, but I thought everyone deserved a time to grieve, and both men deserved to be remembered. Remus died to save Audri's life. Even if he was only a good man for that last ten seconds of his existence, it's enough to say he changed. It's that simple.

Until my next thoughts, I bid adieu.

As Amanda closed the leather-bound book, the ground began to shake, and she could hear the kitchenware rattling in the cabinets.

"Get Jason to the door frame!" she called out to whoever might get to him in time as she scooped Sarina up in her arms and placed herself in the doorway. It was just one of the many earthquakes that had plagued the town lately, and they were getting worse, spreading over a further area. Amanda had become afraid to turn on the news because the center of the earthquake would always be nearby, and she didn't want to hear about it. She wasn't ready to admit fault.

If you enjoyed this sample then look for **Romeo Alpha: A BBW Paranormal Shifter Romance - Book 4**.

Here is a preview of **another story** you may also enjoy:

Devil's Advocate: A BBW MC New Adult Romance Series - Book 4 by Carla Coxwell

KRISTIE MISSED her own bed. It felt like ages since she slept in it. In reality, it had only been three days. She tried telling herself that as she stared up at the hospital ceiling. She ran her fingers over her baby bump. *Not long now,* she thought to herself as she waited for the doctor. But it would be a dangerous final two months until the baby was born.

Severe morning sickness. What was the fancy name the doctor had for it all those months ago? *Hyperemesis Gravidarum.* Kristie could never remember the exact name. All it meant to her was that the violent vomiting she experienced early on wasn't the typical morning sickness. It increased as she got farther along in her pregnancy. She had a particular nasty bout of it this week. Gray begged her to go to the hospital, for the baby's sake so Kristie finally relented.

It was a good thing she did. She was extremely dehydrated. Now she was waiting to hear if she could be released today. Gray said he would be by soon with Megan. He had been to see her this morning but had to go to work.

Kristie closed her eyes, suddenly missing Megan, who was growing so rapidly. It felt like just yesterday that they had taken her in after Kass and Rick were murdered. At the thought of her best friend, Kristie felt a pang in her chest. Her best friend, gunned down by the Infernos, leaving only Megan alive.

Taking in Megan was unexpected. Both Kristie and Gray struggled when they became parents. They had barely taken in Megan when Kristie found out the impossible had happened – she was pregnant. She had given up hope of having a child of her own and had decided that she would focus fully on Megan. The next thing she knew, she was pregnant, vomiting over a toilet bowl while Gray tried to take care of Megan.

Gray handled the news perfectly. For some reason, Kristie was completely terrified that he would be enraged at her pregnancy. They had just taken Megan in and Gray had lost his best friend. But he was overjoyed at the news and slowly, over the course of her pregnancy, he began to change.

In fact, everything would be perfect if it weren't for the Infernos. But wasn't that always the case? Kristie had noticed a shift in Gray, as if he was finally backing away from the gang. But the tendrils of that life refused to fully release Gray. Sometimes Kristie would wake up, having to pee several times a night, and he would be in Megan's room, watching her sleep, lost in thought.

Breaking through her thoughts, the doctor came in to tell her she was going to be released today. Relieved, Kristie called Gray.

<<<>>>

"Thanks for watching her the past few days."

"No problem," Lionel replied, handing Megan over to Gray. "I'm glad we could help."

"I'll have Kristie call Pamela once she gets home."

Lionel nodded and gave a small wave as Gray juggled Megan and all of her things toward the truck. She was fast asleep. She could sleep almost anywhere. Gray envied her as he put her in her car seat. She gave out a soft noise and settled back into her slumber.

Gray got into the driver's seat and headed toward the hospital. He was glad Kristie was coming home. He knew she was going stir crazy in the hospital. He remembered his own time in the hospital and could relate. Being pregnant on top of that must make it even worse.

It was silly but Gray still hadn't fully wrapped his mind around the fact that Kristie was pregnant. It seemed almost unreal to him. They tried for months but there was nothing. Now a baby boy was on the way in two months. Gray glanced back at Megan while stopped at a red light. She was sleeping soundly. She was the perfect mix of Kass and Rick.

His mood turned dark at the thought of his best friend. Gone from this world, struck down by the Infernos. Gray swore revenge for everything Armand had done – shooting Kristie, killing Rick and Kass and leaving Megan an orphan. But the urge for revenge began to fade. With Kristie pregnant and Megan under their care, it seemed selfish to drag out the violence any longer than he already had. If he died, what would happen to Kristie and their two children? Rick had realized he was growing up and was trying to leave the life as well. It seemed foolish not to go.

But leaving the gang was harder than it looked. Even if Gray pulled out of the group and stopped interacting with them, Armand and the Infernos wouldn't let him leave. They would still track him down and hurt him. It was a personal grudge now. They would either kill him or make sure he went to jail for the rest of his life.

So Gray found himself stuck between trying to settle down as a family man and trying to detangle himself from gang life. Kristie had been stressing the importance of communication to him, as if Gray could simply invite Armand out for a cup of tea and settle everything that way.

He pulled into the hospital parking lot. The hospital held such terrible memories for him. He hoped Kristie's pregnancy would offer him something good for a change. He put Megan into her carrier and headed up to get Kristie.

She sat upright in bed. The TV was on some daytime judge show, but her eyes were glazed over from boredom. Her skin was pale, as it had been since her violent morning sickness began. But when Kristie saw him, her eyes lit up.

"Hey," he whispered, pointing to the sleeping Megan.

She nodded and gave a small wave. The discharge procedure took forever and by the time they wheeled Kristie out in her wheelchair, Megan had awakened and was fussing loudly.

"My mom called me right before you came into the room," Kristie said as they headed home. "She wants to come over and help make dinner in the next couple of days. To see how I'm doing."

Gray made a non-committal noise. Things had only mildly improved after they adopted Megan. Pamela, Kristie's mother, wasn't thrilled upon hearing Kristie was pregnant. It made things incredibly awkward for Gray. His uncle was still hung up over the fact Kristie and Gray were cousins. Pamela still blamed him for Kristie's shooting. She was hoping her daughter would divorce him. Being pregnant wasn't part of the plan.

"I think they want to spend more time with Megan," Kristie was saying, not noticing Gray's face. "I said it was fine. Of course I had to say it was fine."

"I understand. They're her grandparents. They'd want to see her."

Kristie nodded, although her facial expression told Gray all he needed to know. She understood how awkward it was for everyone involved.

They arrived home. January snow fell gently. Gray made sure Megan was warm and snug before taking her out of the truck. They headed toward their apartment. Gray thought that even though Kristie had just gotten out of the hospital, she still looked beautiful.

They had moved again. This time to the complex where Rick and Kass used to live. Kass's parents and Gray's own uncle helped out with the rent each month. His uncle said that Pamela helped out as well, but Gray wasn't so sure about that. In any case, with people pitching in to help pay for a bigger apartment, it meant they were able to live in an apartment complex with much better security. It had two bedrooms, unlike their last apartment where Megan's room was non-existent. It was all enclosed which made Kristie feel safer, and was nicer than their last place.

They stepped inside and Kristie scooped up Megan, who badly needed a diaper change and a feeding. Gray offered to help but his words were lost on Kristie, who was giggling and cooing over Megan as usual.

As he watched Kristie tend to Megan and looked around their new apartment, he thought everything had a shot at being perfect. He just had to get out of the Devil's Advocates.

If you enjoyed this sample then look for **Devil's Advocate: A BBW MC New Adult Romance Series - Book 4 by Carla Coxwell**.

Other Books by Darla Dunbar

- The Romeo Alpha BBW Paranormal Shifter Romance Series (This series precedes the "Romeo Alpha Blood Lines Romance Series")

- The Alpha Feud BBW Paranormal Shifter Romance Series

- The Alpha Packed BBW Paranormal Shifter Romance Series

- The Daemon Paranormal Romance Chronicles

- The Mind Talker Paranormal Romance Series

- The Leather Satchel Paranormal Romance Series

Get the latest update on new releases from the author at:

https://darladunbar.com/newsletter/

About the Author - Darla Dunbar

Darla has been interested in paranormal romance since she was a teenager in high school. It was then that she discovered she could fulfill her fantasies through her writing.

Observing people and human behavior in the area of romance has always been one of her favorite pastimes. Combining that with an overactive imagination is a sure fire way of coming up with interesting themes.

Connect with Darla Dunbar

I really appreciate you reading my book! Here are my social media coordinates:

Friend me on Facebook:
https://www.facebook.com/darladunbar/

Follow me on Twitter: https://twitter.com/DarlDunbar

Check me out on Goodreads:
https://www.goodreads.com/author/show/8425857.Darla_Dunbar

Subscribe to my newsletter:
https://darladunbar.com/newsletter/

Visit my website: https://darladunbar.com/

www.ingramcontent.com/pod-product-compliance
Lightning Source LLC
Chambersburg PA
CBHW030815200726
48288CB00004B/1239